THE TUMBLEWEED TWOSOME

Judge Isaac C. Parker had no doubt as to what he was going to do about the sick whiskey runner appearing before him in the dock – hand him ten years in the federal prison at Ohio, and if he died off before the term was up then that was his business.

Only it didn't work out quite that way. One difficulty was the on-and-off nature of the prisoner's illness – and the fact that his sharpness of mind didn't seem to be affected at all by the lung fever.

It took the combined efforts of four deputy U.S. Marshals before Julius Kratoch was finally brought to justice; as well as the profound influence of an ill-treated woman singer they met along the trail ...

THE
TUMBLEWEED
TWOSOME

JEROME GARDNER

A Black Horse Western

ROBERT HALE · LONDON

© Jerome Gardner 1986
First published in Great Britain 1986

ISBN 0 7090 2110 0

Robert Hale Limited
Clerkenwell House
Clerkenwell Green
London EC1R 0HT

Photoset in North Wales by
Derek Doyle & Associates, Mold, Clwyd.
Printed in Great Britain by
St Edmundsbury Press, Bury St Edmunds, Suffolk.
Bound by Hunter & Foulis Ltd.

ONE

It had been a very hot summer indeed down at Fort Smith.

Though the season was still well short of fall, several burned and blistered-looking leaves had dropped from the big jack-oak that grew in the corner of the old stockade, in the original part of the town.

Some of the prematurely shed leaves had scattered over the huge twelve-man gallows that stood nearby the tree. And the death machine itself was showing signs of the day-by-day unremitting heat. Its inventor and principal operative, George Maledon, was up on the platform at this moment, anxiously inspecting the long and deep crack that had first showed on the great crossbeam a month back, and which now stretched almost its full length to where the beam joined the side balks.

He'd tried rubbing in everything he could think of on the bastard: neatsfoot, axle grease, hair oil, even stupid hearsay remedies like milk – all to equal no avail. He was now gloomily resigned to doing the big job of replacing the crossbeam once the summer was past. And meantime he'd just have to tell the Judge that the machine was no longer reliable for the multi-hangings that had made it famous. He certainly wasn't planning to risk his own reputation as the Prince of Hangmen by putting a big weight on that there cracked cross-piece. Dourly, he reached up to make new chalk marks on the split's limits. Since the machine had gotten to cook like this every day the crack was edging on at the rate of about six inches a week.

Up there on the gibbet platform it was even more scorching than on the ground, though it was only ten a.m. The nine steps down shifted loosely under the hangman's boots as he trod them, and the heat on his bare inclined neck was like a flame; it was sheerly crazy not to go out hatted all the time in this sun.

He turned and looked back up at the white-washed, blinding construction for a brief moment before he ran for shade. He mopped his brow with his bandanna and muttered thickly: "Just as well that jigger on today's docket ain't apt to come your way, ol' son ... for I couldn't much as neck-stretch a banty rooster the way I'm feelin' now ..."

The case he referred to was then nearing a conclusion, in the relative cool of the courthouse across the yard.

It was generally regarded as something of a sad case, really; though the concept of a 'sad case' was wholly alien to the large and imposing figure on the bench. To Judge Isaac C. Parker, the so-called Hanging Judge of Arkansas, it was in itself a

straightforward example of yet another whisky-
runner preying on the redmen in the tribal lands to
the west of the county line, which also came under
his jurisdiction where white offenders were concerned.

Julius Kratoch was very definitely one such white
offender. He had been hauled to Fort Smith on no
less than four previous occasions to face the same
charge of introducing spirituous liquors into the
Indian Territories. Only the locations differed; he'd
spread out those former offenses pretty evenly.
First in the Cherokee Nation, then in the Creek
piece, then amongst the Chickasaws and finally in
the Choctaw area. Now, though, he seemed to be
showing a sinister preference for turning the
Choctaws, in particular, into raving madmen in the
wake of his wagon; for he had been stopped with it –
and a hundred kegs – in the main street of
McAlester, and in broad daylight.

Those infuriating facts were of far more moment
to the gravely conscientious judge than was the
equally obvious one that Julius Kratoch was now a
sick man.

The whisky runner had gone down with lung
fever, during the long interval which had elapsed
between his arraignment in this courtroom back in
April and the opening of his trial two days ago. The
Parker court usually convened for six days a week
year round, in an attempt to deal with its heavy
workload; but inevitably there were delays in its
dispensation of justice.

In some ways Julius Kratoch had been fortunate

to spend most of his period of waiting in the relative
comfort of the federal hospital; unlike most other
accuseds who had to kick their heels in the
notorious dungeon underneath the courthouse. But
it was fairly obvious, to the half-dozen relaxed
deputies now guarding the prisoner, that the good
rest and the medics hadn't between them managed
to fix up the hunky's health worth a damn. He still
showed all the classic signs of lung fever: the hot
eyes in the white face, the shallow rattling breath.
He was a whisky peddler who had sold his last
bottle, as everyone in the thinly-attended courtroom was aware. Even Judge Parker had allowed
him to remain seated throughout the trial.

There were no eastern pressmen on hand for this
routine case; they only came down for the more
sensational capital ones. The journalists' bench
boasted just the two sprawled and perspiring
representatives of Fort Smith's own *Elevator* and
Independent. And no more than twenty local
citizens had come inside; more to escape from the
heat than to see the hunky go down. Four of the six
lawmen on trial duty stood in a line with their wet
backs pressed to the big closed entrance doors, and
with their Indian-brown arms folded across
unbuttoned shirt fronts, and their gunbelts sagging
at full notch. The other two guards stood beside the
prisoner, occasionally swaying from one cramped
leg to the other.

The folds of the national flag stirred a very little
beside Isaac Parker as he began his summation of
the case. There was a large window open behind

him that evidently permitted the entry of a faint breeze; though there was not the slightest indication of it otherwise in the oven-like torpid atmosphere. The other windows, along one length of the courtroom, were also adjusted open to their fullest extent; and just as uselessly. Now and then the sick man in the dock would cast a glance out of the nearest side aperture, looking at freedom with a glazed apathy while his shoulders continued to rise and fall with that pitiable morbid quickness.

Judge Parker was no less hot than anybody else, and he saw no reason to drag this matter out beyond its essentials. However, as he ended his directions to the jury he felt bound to give them a final word of warning in this case. Fixing his intensely blue gaze on each member in turn he grated:

"Gentlemen, there is a natural tendency to feel an impulse toward extending leniency to the prisoner who stands – umm, I should say who sits before you." He gave a sardonic smile. "Indeed, if any of us did not feel that for ourselves at the outset of this trial, the learned counsel for the defense was at some pains to ensure that those emotions were properly awoken." He paused again and frowned with his heavy brows.

"I used that word advisedly, gentlemen: *emotions*. It is only right that we should indulge them, to a degree, for one whom Almighty God has seen fit to punish in advance of your own verdict ...

"And yet, does that imply we should be any less feeling in our attitude to those several citizens of the Indian Territory, who, according to the tenor of the government's argument, and also to many of its witnesses who have appeared before you, the prisoner Kratoch had 'callously left behind him in a wake of destruction,' to quote from Mr Clayton's final address to you?"

The jurist's voice was suddenly loud and impassioned in the hot room. "I think not, gentlemen. *Their* welfare is most definitely your prior concern. Julius Kratoch has received every possible attention from the government's doctors here at Fort Smith since his illness was first detected. His present condition is *not the point at issue.* I cannot stress that too strongly. I direct that you are to regard his crime – if you deem he has in fact committed one – entirely as if it were perpetrated by a man enjoying the fullest health and vigor. And now I commend you all to the guidance of the Almighty in your earnest deliberations on His behalf."

* * *

Deputy marshal Alvin Simmons, stationed midway of the line of four lawmen lolling on the courthouse doors, waited until the jurymen were shuffling outside before remarking quietly to Deputy Stu Morris beside him: "Never knowed the old cuss to talk of God save at a hangin' case. Kind of funny, don't you think?"

"Ah: but then you never saw a red-eye merchant so close to God as that hunky is, Al. And I'd allow that Isaac ain't neither. Why, you only got to lookit him to see he's like a haystack burnin' out in a gale. I sure cain't keep my own thoughts off of God when I lookit him, I know that."

"You think he'll draw a hitch in Ohio?" put in the guard on Simmons's other side, Bobby Halleck.

"Nah. Waste of a railroad voucher. Isaac'll jes' stuff him downstairs for a week or so. Tha's all it'll need."

*   *   *

The jury filed back in at eleven-fifteen, and the experienced defense attorney, J. Warren Reed, knew at once from their faces that his eloquence had been wasted.

He didn't feel he could blame them; or that the Judge had misdirected them any more than was customary in his religious zeal to obtain a conviction. For apart from developing lung fever Julius Kratoch had given him a pretty hopeless hand to deal on his behalf. In contrast with the lay opinions of the guard deputies, the shrewd lawyer now thought to himself: *That old buzzard will hand him ten years back east – even if he only does ten days of it.*

Kratoch himself was obviously quite indifferent to the building tension all around him as the jury foreman stood to give the verdict. However he did seem to think that the climax of the proceedings against him meant that he himself should stand, even though incapacitated. Ignoring the restraining gesture of the guard on his right side he struggled pathetically upward and shifted forward to grasp hold of the dock rail, and to face Judge Parker with a sort of feeble resolution.

That new position brought his wasted right cheek into a harsh swatch of sunlight from the nearest side-window, and again he glanced that way with vacant wistfulness.

"Well, Mr Foreman?" Isaac Parker asked briskly. "And what is –?"

There was a sudden blur of movement from the prisoner. At first, largely because of the impression he had made from his initial appearance in the courtroom, many of the court officials and spectators merely got an impression that he'd fallen forward in a sudden collapse.

But that wasn't so. Julius Kratoch had indeed moved forward; but under full and rapid control of his limbs. He had used his hold on the dock rail to vault nimbly over it, landing atop of the large and solid exhibits table which stood between the dock and the bench.

Most of the table surface at that end was occupied by several big glass jars, containing samples of the reddish and smoky-looking liquid that had once again caused the prisoner to renew his acquaintance with Judge Parker. He hit down amongst them with his solid flat-heel boots, wobbling and thrashing wildly as the glassware rolled and broke up beneath him, but somehow keeping his balance as he launched himself onward and upward straight for the figure behind the bench. Some raw whiskey from his trampling had splashed up and wetted Parker's astounded face.

Neither of the two deputies who had been flanking him had as much as twitched a muscle yet. What with the great heat, and their by now total relaxation around the mortally sick booze trader, his break had come as just as much a surprise and shock to them as it had to everyone else in the paralysed courtroom.

That long moment of paralysis and incomprehension was taken full advantage of by the prisoner. The bench itself rose a daunting five feet above floor level, but the height of the exhibits table more than halved that as Kratoch lurched off the broken glass and clawed his way up to stand, for a split second, actually above the still seated jurist, on the edge of his long desk.

There then followed a spectacle which, in the opinion of many, outshone anything that had ever gone before it at the United States District Court for Western Arkansas.

Several things happened together to make up that spectacle; so that subsequently nobody was quite able to agree as to the exact sequence.

One detail was absolutely certain, however: the prisoner definitely paused in his break attempt while he coughed blood over both Judge Parker and the flag on its pole beside him. Presumably that enforced delay in his escape plan was brought on by his exertions in getting thus far. That point was verifiable by means of the red-flecked flag he left behind him, to say nothing of the Judge's spoiled Washington suit.

Then the timing became confused, as almost all the other people in the courtroom finally became as wide awake as Julius Kratoch. All six of the guards were at last lunging for their revolvers, not too swiftly in the main, since their positions had been arranged more to accommodate a heat wave than to stop an escaper. And when all their draws were eventually made, Kratoch had by then made it very daunting and difficult for them to cut him down: by placing one of his boots calmly on Isaac Charles Parker's white-haired cranium ...

That final, outrageous, preposterous act on the part of the prisoner at last broke the Judge's spell of dumbfoundment, which had lasted longer that anyone else's. He surged wrathfully upright to his full six feet; which unfortunately only served to hoist Julius Kratoch more in the direction he'd been planning to take since soon after his trial opened. As Parker raised him up, the whiskey runner tensed with his judge-based leg and kicked himself off him, to tumble through the window in back of the high bench.

He didn't manage to go through it cleanly; there was a further jangle of glass as a big pane was broken. But he went out quite well enough.

Then the court was in pandemonium. As soon as Kratoch had cleared the Judge, the air all around him was thick with pursuing bullets. Isaac Parker, beside himself with rage, ignored the flying lead and rushed over to the aperture after the prisoner, heaving himself up bodily against the wall there to peer out.

His physical effort was rewarded by the sight of Julius Kratoch sprinting across the gravel yard toward the large grulla horse which he had been observing earlier through the side window. The animal had been left tethered helpfully to a section of the stockade fence.

The Judge jerked his head around to bawl to his lawmen to get out there; but the main group of four by the doors had done that already. They spilled and tumbled down the courthouse steps, shooting wildly from the hip as they came.

Gravel chips spurted up around the hunky's speeding feet; but he was fast going out of range by that time. Also, a combination of dust and heat haze was roiling about him in a protective pall. Nothing appeared to hit either him or the startled grey as he skinned aboard it, and jerked the tie rope off the paling.

The big gate hadn't been left open; but that didn't much reassure most of the now kneeling-and-aiming deputies, who well knew what Bailiff Hardy's gelding was capable of. Either the sly hunky must have somehow discovered that for himself, or else was acting now out of sheer horse-instinct honed by desperation, for he spun that rawboned jughead on a dime and then put it straight at the fence, suicidally close ...

But the bailiff's animal was quite unbothered. It took off in a buck that crashed itself and the whiskey runner down in a jarring heap on the far side. Then, amidst the crash of their final volley, they heard Kratoch's cough-broken yell as he began frenziedly kicking at the grey's slats.

Probably those bare-heeled boots of his weren't enough to set it a-running; probably it just wanted to run anyway, like it most always seemed to want to do whenever Bailiff Hardy nerved himself to get up on it; which wasn't all that often.

Whatever the reason, it now ran – at a raking dead gallop in the westerly direction of the Poteau River.

TWO

It was the kind of luckless affair which got no better at all as it unfolded.

After the apoplectic Judge had adjourned the proceedings, Bailiff Hardy was instructed to wait on him immediately in his private chambers.

Isaac Parker then soon learned that it was only because the normally conscientious bailiff had come in late that morning that he had hastily hitched his animal to the paling on his way in, instead of leaving it in its usual stall in the government stable. The bailiff lived some distance out of town. Like quite a few others on the skimpy federal payroll, Hardy was primarily a local farmer who moonlighted some court work.

"I see ..." Parker ground out in the tone of one who was seeing – or at any rate sympathizing – very little. "Well, I suppose there's one thing I should be grateful for even after what's happened: at least that confounded bronco of yours didn't have a rifle on the saddle, which would very likely have been so if he'd happened to take one of the deputies' mounts. Kratoch will be unarmed, wherever he now is. That gives the substantial force which has been

sent after him every chance to recapture him
without further incident."

The bailiff's eyes dropped away from the Judge's
and he visibly squirmed. He coughed a little and
said: "It's true I ain't no deppity, Y'r Honor, but –"
He broke off and gave a nervous swallow.

The Judge stiffened and glared. "*But what*,
Hardy?"

"Well, the thing is, Y'r Honor, I rid in this
morning by way of my north meadow, see …"

"Is that of any consequence?"

"Well, yeh, Y'r Honor, I guess it is at that. The
thing is I been plagued with gophers in that
meadow and so I –" He met the hard judicial stare
a shade too head-on, and his throat dried on him
again.

Isaac Parker was no agriculturist, but his mind
was accustomed to deducing probable facts from
known premises. He now said with considerable
bitterness: "So you did have a gun on that dratted
creature … What kind of a gun?"

Hardy worked up what was intended as an
apologetic grin, then hastily ironed it out when he
saw how it was received. "Uh, it was my old
scattergun, Judge."

"Ah, but then perhaps it was empty of loads after
you had, umm, despatched the gophers?" the jurist
suggested patiently and in a more hopeful tone.

Hardy's close-shaven head dipped down lower
still where he was standing. "Sure, the gun was
empty."

"Splendid! What a relief!"

"'Cepting I had ten boxes of Double-O in the saddlepouch. Y'see the thing was I was fixing to give 'em another few blasts on my way home, to catch the few you allus get that's cagier than the rest and pops up after you gone by."

There followed a rather unpleasant further exchange between the two of them; so unpleasant that it was a positive relief to the bailiff when the Judge's personal clerk knocked on the door and said: "Time for you to see Colonel Hall now, sir."

Hardy scurried gratefully past the Colonel's trim military figure in the doorway; feeling grateful, too, that his handy court job hadn't actually been taken away from him over that lousy zebra horse, which he'd always known was trying to do for him one way or another. He hoped fervently that the escaped hunky lived long enough to take it far away from him, so that he'd never see it again.

Colonel Hall, the U.S. marshal at Fort Smith who was in charge of the two-hundred-strong force of field deputies, eyed the choleric figure of the Judge with due caution.

Naturally he knew all about what had happened earlier in and outside the courthouse. And he thought that he had a fair idea of how the coming conversation would go. He hadn't been looking forward to it any more keenly than had the bailiff before him.

"Ah, Henry ... have you got him yet? Sit down, man, sit down ..."

The marshal undid a button on his light Chesterfield and perched uneasily where he was bidden. Despite the heat he was dressed as formally as ever. Sunlight bounced off his tight brown boots, though unable to add much to their West Point glitter.

"Alas no, Isaac. As luck would have it the ferry was in the slip when he got to the Poteau. It appears he had a riot gun on that grey and –"

"So I have gathered already. Did he kill the ferryman?"

The colonel smoothed his drooping white mustache. "No. He just peppered shot into the barge and made old John dance a bit. Then he saw fit to pole him across. One can hardly blame him. Of course I've told the posse to keep going for as long as it takes, but I think it has to be faced that with that much start he'll soon be deep in the Choctaw hills. Probably the Sansbois. Or else the Winding Stairs. Or I suppose he might go on down to the Kiamichi country. I understand from his record that was where he brewed his poison most times, along the Kiamichi headwaters."

"But thunderation, man, he can't last long enough to get there! Just take a look at this suit of mine! See – that's lung blood. He could fall off that confounded horse at any moment! Doctor Taylor has just been assuring me of that likelihood."

The marshal pulled at his earlobe in a way that expressed a plain man's scepticism of that kind of certainty in a case like this. He murmured: "I've been in a few posses myself, Isaac. It's sheerly astounding how long they tend to keep a quarry in the saddle. I'm mindful of one chase in particular, on the Trinity it was, when we were running the track of some hill boy who'd killed his cousin – or some such usual affair where he came from. Y'know, that boy was shot to bits in the first mile of running him. Yet still he out-rode us clear from the Ozarks to the Trinity. And then he somehow slipped us, and by then, I tell you, we'd had enough. That's the point of this little story: we'd had enough and he hadn't. Oh, Taylor's a good medic, I know that. But I doubt if he's ever been run by a posse himself," he concluded forcefully.

The Judge sat gloomily silent for a moment. He had sent too many posses in his time into the wilder regions of the Indian Territory to have much faith in them. Not only for the kind of reason that the old soldier beside him had put forward, but because he'd learned that on those occasions when a posse *did* catch up with a fugitive they tended to become over-excited by their achievement; and feel inclined to substitute a cottonwood for the Fort Smith gallows. No, he was no believer in posses. It had merely seemed expedient to send one after Julius Kratoch, in the expectation of them retrieving his corpse a mile or so from the state line. Now, both the marshal's cautionary tale and his own instinct were telling him it wouldn't be that simple.

He said finally: "Umm. He certainly must have had a bit more strength than anyone realized to get free as he did." His face flushed up as he re-lived those stupefying moments earlier in the day, and he looked angrily at the dapper figure across his desk.

He was annoyed that they had slipped into their usual Christian-name terms at this meeting, and spoke next with the determination of setting their talk on a proper level of stern reproof.

"Marshal Hall, I require an explanation from you for the disgracefully lax attitude shown by the court guards today. Those men inside were half-asleep, and there should have been several others posted out in the square as we had to have the windows open on account of this abominable heat. Why were those elementary precautions not taken?" he demanded, with a flash of the famous deepset blue eyes.

"I can give an explanation, though hardly an excuse, Judge," Hall responded with matching stiffness. He had known the whip would be cracked over him sooner or later, once the civilities were done with. "The men were drowsy and it was, as you say, very hot. They – and I must confess that goes for me too – were lulled by that hunky's half-dead looks. Otherwise I would have had more men outside the buildings."

His own face had grown slightly pink by now, and he continued a little more sharply: "And after all, how could anyone guess that he would have the all-fired gall to ..." But he decided to let the end of that sentence go unsaid.

"To stand on his judge's head in order to effect an exit?" Isaac Parker supplied icily. "I gather you are cognizant of that detail of the escape?"

The marshal nodded, while holding his features to a careful gravity. He had in fact laughed a good deal amongst his deputies when that choice aspect of it was retailed to him. "Er, precisely, Judge. But I don't think we should conclude from that that he's faked his illness. No one could look as he did and not be truly ailing. But he probably cozened Taylor and the rest of them that he was a sight worse than he really is at this stage of it. I was around lung fever a lot in the Army, and some of those lungers were also malingerers at times. If I don't miss my guess this one will lose that posse in the Sansbois without too much trouble."

"Then pull them back," the Judge barked with sudden authority. "Send a man after them and get them back here."

Colonel Hall was astonished by this apparent turnaround. "Very well ... but I had the impression you wanted to see Kratoch in court again pretty damn badly."

Isaac Parker was too preoccupied at that moment to rebuke the swearing in his presence as he would normally have felt bound to do. He murmured: "That impression is correct. I want you to get a wagon team together. Two or three of your best men and a driver. Tell them to go after Kratoch – and only Kratoch. Tell them I want him if it takes them ten years of trailing. And make it quite clear that if I see their faces back here without that confounded Bohemian's as well, they're off the force."

Hall grunted. The quiet intensity of that order had left him in no more doubt as to the Judge's strength of purpose over Kratoch. But there were some practical objections to his new plan that he felt he must raise.

"The men concerned won't be best pleased if they can't fill the cage with other prisoners while they're in the Territory. As of course you know, they receive arrest money on top of mileage allowance for a normal tumbleweed run. For that matter, why does it have to be a full-blown wagon for only one man? Why not just let them take an extra pack nag along?"

The Judge's harsh cast of features now softened in the disconcerting way it sometimes did.

"Because Kratoch is ill. I am not forgetting that despite his – his unique method of absconding from justice," he declared firmly. "He must be given the relative comfort of an uncrowded conveyance for his return here. There is also the question of possible infection. It therefore follows that no other men are to travel with him in the prisoner wagon. I charge you to see that is carried out to the letter, Marshal. And in view of what you say as to the pecuniary considerations which influence some deputies, I think you should call for volunteers for this assignment; find the stamp of man who wants to do this job for its own sake, Henry, rather than for any specific reward. Though you may let it be known that I shall view the future prospects of *successful* volunteers very favorably," he added with a compromising sigh. He had a fair idea by now of what he could, and could not, ask for from his workaday body of lawmen.

Colonel Hall was still of the opinion that he was asking a sight too much now. "High class volunteers ... for no arrest money," he said wryly. "Well, I'll do my best. But there's another difficulty in what you have in mind. A tumbleweed wagon won't be able to go high enough in those rock mountains if that's where he is. If they catch him high up in one or other of the Choctaw range he'll have to be brought down on horseback, sick or not."

The Judge squared his broad shoulders in a resolute way that had discouraged many a defendant. "Then in those circumstances the wagon must be taken as far up as possible, to afford Kratoch every comfort that we can." He eyed his military subordinate with a return to dour formality. "Those are my instructions to you, Marshal Hall. Recall the posse and make ready a team of able volunteers to send out shortly with a prisoner wagon. Good afternoon to you."

* * *

There weren't a great many deputies knocking around Fort Smith at this or any other time. Judge Parker didn't believe in exposing any more of them to the temptations of The Row and Cocaine Hill than was strictly necessary as occasional relaxation from their arduous duties in the rest of Western Arkansas and the Indian Territory. And of the men who were then in town, a good percentage had taken off with the posse after the escaped prisoner.

So Colonel Hall decided to do nothing for the moment. But when the first of the recalled riders clattered up First Street and then dismounted by

the office to claim his posse fee, he saw that a new
notice had been pinned up with the others by the
door there.

The posseman read it, and was soon joined by
another one and then by several others.

"*Shee-it*," Marv Pollins said explosively. "A
tumbleweed run jes' for that lousy hunky? Totin'
an empty cage 'cepting for him inside coughin' his
guts up ... What kind of fandango is that? Ain't
nothin' in it for nobody. The colonel can go shove
that one up his asshole."

Doug Martin said in a more thoughtful tone: "I
don't know so much about there bein' nothing in it.
See the end bit? *The peace officers responsible for
the safe and unharmed return of the prisoner to
custody can look forward to assured preferment in
their future careers of law enforcement.*"

"Whatinhell does that mean?"

"It means the old judge is on fire to grab aholt of
that hunky for shinnin' up him the way he did,"
Bobby Ross put in sagely.

"It don't say that much," Pollins objected. "All
it says is 'assewered preferment.' Preferment's the
same as sayin' preferred, ain't it? So what's being
assewered preferred accordin' to that paper?"

"The colonel, he sure as hell prefers to see
someone else's ass but his gettin' filled with the
hunky's buckslugs," suggested Harry Dason ingeni-
ously. But before that theory could be discussed the
U.S. marshal's immaculately groomed white head
came around the door, and silence fell upon the
group until he spoke.

"Well, then? Did you pick him off the ground before I brought you back?"

"No, sir, Colonel. He made it past them screed-over footslopes," Dason told him. "That bailiff's nag was still goin' like a train over the stones. If you hadn't turned us around I'm scared we'd have lost him anyway by night time. We'd have needed us an Injun along to foller him over the rock."

"Hm. I see ... Well, I expect some of you have read this by now." Hall tapped the new notice. Almost the entire posse had now got down at the nearby hitching rail and been joined by several loafing deputies who hadn't gone out with them, but who were now curious to learn the outcome of the pursuit. The colonel pitched up his voice heartily to include them all.

"Well, boys? Who's going to be the first volunteer to bring that troublesome bohunk back here in a tumbleweed?"

THREE

Nothing could have been more deafening than the next few seconds of silence; or less enthusiastic than the bunch of faces turned warily to his.

Not that he was at all surprised. Isaac Parker's lofty notions of career advancement, and so forth, just didn't mean much to men who were primarily hungry for scalp money and the chance to spend it in deadfalls or on The Row. He stroked his white mustache, reflecting that it was fortunate there were other ways and means, apart from incentives, for keeping a body of troops in line; even a slovenly lot of semi-civilians like the specimens here now, the colonel reflected moodily.

No doubt *his* way couldn't be counted on to find the high calibre of hunky hunter that the Judge had in mind for the job. But that couldn't be helped. He smiled upon them and said genially: "Well, I'll leave you to think it over, boys. Now, file inside for the posse money – singly, please. Each man only one at a time."

While they had been absent on the posse he'd thoughtfully gone through the files of those men who weren't presently out in the field. While doing so he had tried to bear in mind what the Judge would look for in a candidate for 'preferment', while hard-headedly looking out also for any interesting flaws of character that there might be in the records. He had six names jotted down tentatively on his blotter when the first posseman came in to be paid.

Joey Higdon wasn't one of that six. And neither was the next one in line, Tom Halliday. (Though he almost put it to Tom, suddenly recalling that deputy's well-known aversion to mid-Europeans like Kratoch. But then he also remembered Parker's strange insistence on showing kindness to the runaway and so he closed his mouth and let Halliday go on out.)

But then Bill Cramer stepped up to the desk. Cramer was on his short list. He paid him and said: "Ah, Cramer … be seated for one moment." His left hand went out to Cramer's file and turned it open.

Cramer was a deputy whose wife had left him for a young dry-goods salesman a year ago. He had spent a fair amount of time in jail since then; but he was basically a good experienced man. He rarely smiled nowadays. He had a still livid scar down one impassive cheek, acquired before his last interment of ninety days below the courthouse.

Colonel Hall now mused in a sorrowful style: "How long are you apt to stay amiable this time, Bill?" He motioned at the paper in front of him. "Seems to me that unless you're kept permanently out in the field you're just set and determined on trouble."

He eyed him in a sympathetic, square way. "I'm not bothered personally, you understand. I know you to be a dedicated peace officer at heart. But *the Judge*, now, you know how strictly he feels about any member of the force getting into regular scraps of his own ... Y'know, a file like this one has become, a file we could call *deteriorating*, would cause him a great deal of distress, Cramer ... were he to see it."

Bill Cramer was thirty-two years old and a government deputy for ten of them. He glanced at Colonel Hall, nodded a few times to himself, and then said flatly: "You want me for this cheap tumbleweed run. OK I'll do it."

Hall gazed at him earnestly. "Well, as a matter of fact it did occur to me that if you were to be involved with Kratoch's safe recovery, especially if you were senior man along ..." He gestured again at the file. "A lot of this would seem very superficial criticism in the light of such an achievement. Why, I question that it would seem relevant enough to stay on your record at all."

"I'd rod the team, uh ..." Cramer muttered with supreme indifference. He gave a sudden and startling grin which quite altered his sombre face for just a brief second. "Don't that hang any on who else, uh, volunteers for it?"

"Not really," Hall replied smoothly. "Since I only have in mind to invite younger men to go with you. Or at any rate no-one much older."

Cramer shrugged. "Like I say I'll do it anyway," he repeated in what was now his usual remote, bitter manner. He got up and took his money and left.

*   *   *

A few minutes later it was Marvin Pollins's turn to be paid off for his short spell of federal endeavour. This time, after Colonel Hall had said: "Ah, Pollins, just a moment," he was not quite so sure how best to proceed.

The boy hadn't done anything wrong much; he was just a loudmouth who drank too much down in the colored bars. And there was a certain girl working on First Street who kept telling her customers that she had been promised the heady position of Mrs Pollins until Marvin turned queasy on the notion very late. But Hall only knew of that through keeping his ear open to town gossip. There was only the drinking actually down on file. But, of course, Pollins wouldn't know that. He now decided to shuffle it around some.

"Of course you know how His Honor feels about drunken immorality, Pollins. I'm sure there's no need for me to spell that out to you. And when it's compounded by causing a good woman to take to a Life of Shame ... well, it's hard to see how a man's friends could stand by him if a thing like that were to be widely known ... officially known. You do take my point, Pollins?"

In fact young Marv, a young twenty-two, didn't take the point nearly as fast as Cramer had, and the marshal had to goad him patiently for several more minutes until he began to appreciate the positive advantages of joining the tumbleweed team.

As the youth stepped bemusedly out of the office, Hall told himself that he'd make out pretty well under a solid man like Bill Cramer. He knew Pollins to be steady and accurate with a carbine, and, as a Missourian, most likely also a dependable man with mules. That last was an important point: for if a prisoner wagon was to be hauled around in mountain country they were going to need mules.

Slim Huttman was pressured in a way that caused a certain amount of private shame even to the hard-boiled old soldier; the leverage being applied mainly through Huttman's recently bullet-busted left leg. Both Judge Parker and himself had lost faith in him as a horsebacker, Slim now learned. Also, that he was plumb lucky there was a driving job going for the asking until the leg healed – even if it did have to be over hurtful and jarring terrain like the Sansbois.

But Slim didn't delay in falling into line. The only other job he knew was cows, and he had an ex-cowhand's deep-rooted terror of being forced back to it while stove up.

The last man that Hall discussed the job with in further detail was Paul Monkerud. He hadn't been out with the posse and Hall sent for him, after a good deal of hesitation, when the pay-out was over.

Monkerud was well named, for he was subject to occasional bouts of fundamentalist passion that were always very violent and had at least once been fatal. As a youngster Monkerud had strangled a co-religionist in Kansas, and only a few weeks back he had gone on a shooting spree in The Row: when cold sober and acting only as a passive instrument of the Lord's Will. However, and paradoxically, Monkerud was also a first-class lawman with several brave and hazardous arrests to his credit.

Colonel Hall now lectured him vaguely about his past misdeeds, without much noticeable effect. The bedrock of the zealot's sullen resistance to the idea was his strong liking for money. Hall had come across that combination with religious fanaticism before during his long career with the military, and now with Judge Parker's private army.

A tumbleweed without a full cage in back simply wasn't Monkerud's notion of worthwhile peace-keeping; and he was not the kind of man to be manipulated by normal means. Furthermore he was well aware that his actual work record was second to none, and that Isaac Parker was unlikely to fire a fellow Believer whatever this old brass-hat went and told him.

But then Hall had come up with a rather inspired suggestion that if he agreed to join the team he might get to Julius Kratoch just in time to do something for his immortal soul – a task plainly beyond the capacity of sorry heathens like Cramer, Pollins and Huttman. And after a long stubborn pause, the thin and expressionless Monkerud had given a resigned nod of compliance.

The colonel beamed with relief. He was fairly confident that Bill Cramer would be able to keep Monkerud hogged down from the period while they were out. He sensed that in an odd way those two were like fire and water, now that Cramer had changed so much. He had picked Monkerud to go especially because of his tracking ability, which was as weirdly good as any Yaqui's. He knew that it would need to be, too, following a cold trail in places like the Winding Stairs.

And that was the best the U.S. marshal had been able to do at short notice, given the obvious necessity to arrange a fairly prompt pursuit of Julius Kratoch before he either died off or his trail died right out or else he somehow survived and ran outside the court's jurisdiction. As an outfit, he was aware that Parker might have been disappointed with those he'd selected. The only one of them with a trace of unselfishness in his make-up happened to be a religious-crazed, warped-minded killer who had only escaped the noose because of his tender years at the time. The rest were all more or less lazy, inefficient, profane, grudge bearing, dollar hunting, boozing, fornicating, typical federal deputies …

He just had to hope it would somehow work out.

*   *   *

"Look, if that damn spook Monk is goin' then I ain't!"

"We need a top tracker for those rock hills," Cramer said boredly, shifting a wad of chewing plug from his scarred cheek to the other side.

He and Pollins were at the large government stable, seeing the liveryman there about supplies for the run. Huttman and Monkerud were outside in the as yet cool yard, selecting a prisoner wagon from the four vehicles that were not then in use.

"So why not chouse up an Injun?" Marv Pollins was saying now. "The spook can't be no slicker than an Injun."

Cramer seemed to ignore that, looking up from checking the equipment end of their chuck box but only to gaze past Pollins's short stocky frame. Ab Fosser, the liveryman, had put in three sets of irons instead of the four they would need. He bawled: "*Ab!*" and then resumed in his former weary tone: "You may not know it but in fact Paul is some better than most Indians I ever saw at follerin' over rocks. Anyway, slack off – I didn't pick him, the colonel did. You don't like it you go and tell him."

When Fosser came over to them from the tack room he said to him coldly: "We'se four on this trip, not three. One more set of eatin' tools … And while you're here I ain't too happy with them sacks of flour. They got a stale look to me."

"Stale! They ain't stale, they been here under a week!" the liveryman snorted. Then he caught Cramer's experienced eye and shrugged a little. "Well, now I think on it they could of been left from that other load. Right, I'll change 'em."

"Thanks. I'll need to check the harness next. And put up some more canned stuff. Like I said, there's four of us goin' out for I dunno how long."

"Seems you figger we'll be travellin' a good piece,

then, after this half-dead hunky," Marv Pollins said in a wondering way.

Cramer ejected a brown stream at the wide drain channel in the floor. "Hard to tell. He seems purty spry by some accounts don't he."

"You mean the way he runned up the ol' judge! Jesus, I only wisht I'd been on court guard that day and seed the bugger do it, I surely do!"

"Yeh. While you're talkin', check that leather-mending set Fosser put out. On the bale there. And don't forget to look the mules over before we hitch up – I'm countin' on you for that. Huttman ain't no hand around mules like you wouldn't expect him to be," Cramer said quietly.

He was already growing slightly impatient with Pollins, and realized that didn't bode too well for their relationship on the trip. But, along with almost every other irritation in the post-wife arid existence of William Cramer, he didn't care particularly whether Pollins annoyed him or not.

Outside, Slim Huttman was going over the rig he had finally chosen, in company with the black-smith. Slim knew all four tumbleweeds only too well. This bastard he'd picked was just about the best bastard, which was all he could say for it. The onetime cowhand limped around it with scowling care, then halted to stoop awkwardly down and jab a finger behind the rear nighside wheel.

"That box goes hot. I know from my last time out, which was with this damn thing. We got bogged in them Chickasaw redlands, and she went hot as hell on us every time we stuck."

"I saw to that since then, I'm almost sure," the blacksmith grumbled, hunkering to look from the wagon's other side.

"Make me quite sure by seein' to it now," Huttman grunted acidly, straightening.

He wasn't usually snippy this way. Months of hurting in this heat had changed his usual placid disposition. His leg was still quite painful even after this long since it was shot. The bullet hadn't been picked out fast enough. It was in him too badly to be tried for by the other men on the run, and had stayed in until they struck a Chickasaw mission and the doc there had finally dug and chipped it loose. It had gone a bit bad by then, and losing the lead hadn't stopped the poison from spreading inside the torn bone – so the Fort docs had said when he finally got back.

And plainly that hard luck streak wasn't over ... It was about to turn him into that lowest form of lawman life known as a tumbleweed driver. And with mules, for God's sake. To say nothing of being cookie and fire-pit digger, as always went with the job.

Slim now gave vent to a vague sort of cuss that was meant to include Isaac Charles Parker, Henry Maitland Hall, his more humble self, his paining leg, and also that so-called Mad Monk he would soon have to ride with; now standing stiffly across the yard with his back to the pole corral.

Paul Monkerud's figure, long in itself, cast a giant pencil of a shadow in the early sunlight, reaching almost over to the group of parked wagons. He really did look crazy, Slim thought suddenly. It wasn't just imagined, from what the other boys were always saying about him. He had never been parded with him before and surely didn't admire being so now. From what he'd heard it would mean Bible readings every suppertime, with the alternative of a crazy run-in with the man if you told him what to do.

"Holy shit," he growled morosely; with a slow unwilling grin as it came to him that he'd sworn something precisely fitting that time.

FOUR

Slim Huttman tooled the rig down to the Poteau
ferry and went over with it alone. The stocked-up
tumbleweed weighed a good deal, with its solid
running gears and heavy log chain in the cage
section, and it sank the barge below its load line as
it crossed. Then Huttman waited on the Territory
side while the ferryman re-crossed to pick up the
mules and the three horsebackers.

Bill Cramer sat a lineback dun that seemed to
share his own disgusted outlook on life. The
short-sized, almost squat shape of Marv Collins
was aboard a claybank that looked bigger than it
was under that particular burden. And Paul
Monkerud was like a vertical dark appendage of the
sooty-colored animal that was his personal horse.
The other mounts, including the extra tied behind
the wagon, were government stock.

They hitched up again and began to climb the
gradual grade that led to the Sansbois on that
eastern side of the mountains. For a while, Fort
Smith danced and swam behind them in the
building heat as the inevitable sun of this endless

41

summer rose to its position of full blast.

They made a brief camp at noon where the posse had left a marker jammed in a large spillage of rocks at the foot of the abrupt upthrust of the mountains themselves. Slim Huttman boiled coffee beside a burned out mountain creek which expired finally in little more than a dampness through the scree. The four of them crouched together in a small bowl they had cleared in the field of granite debris, where the water ran a bit stronger.

The overhanging rock battlements were already having a sobering effect as they gulped down the coffee and chewed at a saddlebag lunch. Huttman grumbled: "The old judge don't know what he's asking, sendin' a full-blowed prisoner rig up there." The ex-cowhand's gaze shifted over to where the mules and saddlestock were plucking at brown grass growing amid mangled-looking thornbrush on the edge of the rock field. "I know somethin' else – we'll be hollerin' for a blacksmith after an hour or so up that face."

"Maybe not. There's a track of a kind goes up behind that big chimney rock," Cramer murmured, pointing with one hand while he dabbed his neckpiece at his sweating face with the other. "I guess the hunky could of flown up that way. I went up there myself a few years back after ... some character I can't even recall his name now. All this was awash then, rollin' stones down like dice. Hell of a change now."

That was quite a long speech for the withdrawn wife-loser to come out with. But it didn't much surprise Paul Monkerud, who had ridden on a previous occasion with the head deputy since Helen Cramer had quit western Arkansas with her new drummer companion. Monkerud knew that Cramer did tend to come a bit more to life again when he was out on the job.

The sombre-faced religious zealot was a close observer of his fellow lawmen, without generally much understanding them. He now came slowly to his full six feet plus and said in his deep-throated, concise, always somehow crosswise manner: "He may not have gone over the top at all. I have a feeling not. I'll find out directly."

He checked his handgun as he began to move off, dropping his empty tin cup contemptuously by Huttman as he passed him and began clambering over the scree toward the chimney rock.

"Jesus I can't stand that motherfucker," Marv Pollins announced not over-loudly as Monkerud moved out of earshot. "Though why that's so I dunno a fuck."

Slim's weathered and pain-tightened face suddenly cracked into a hard grin. "You speak straight out to Monk the style you favor, sonny, and happen you'll find out why pretty quick."

"That's true," Cramer grunted thoughtfully as he tossed his own cup over. "Marv, you cinch in your language while this run lasts, or Paul will be nigh impossible to live with. You better believe that."

"I ain't running scared of that spook," the younger man said sullenly. "He can take me any whichaway he damn pleases." He got up and began to lurch and wobble back to the wagon.

"I guess the heat's getting to that one: though he still seems awful young for twenny-two, don't he," Huttman complained as he began breaking camp. "The idee of him and Monk forever lock-hornin' in them hills, till Lord knows when we find the hunky if ever – it don't give me any pleasure at all, William, I tell you."

"Looks like you could be getting in a stew for nothin' as to that," Cramer told him with a jerk of his head. "Paul's not sniffing up that path I mentioned. See, he's going north along the edge there."

The driver twisted around, catching his breath as that effort caught his bad leg. He shaded his eyes, seeing that the tall dark figure was indeed now stepping along the base of the rockface.

Both the head deputy and the driver knew that Monkerud was highly trustworthy in that single respect. Huttman said explosively: "*Godamighty* ... if we'd only kept on goin' a bit farther in that posse we'd of had the hunky in no time! Seems to me he must of fogged it behind that lookout rock, like to fool us, then dove back to the grass again by the long spur ridge that leads off there." He stood up and pointed excitedly.

Cramer shrugged, taking in his shellbelt as he came upright. "Or the bailiff's bronco did, more probably. Last I saw of Kratoch yesterday he was no more than a horse-backin' corpse."

"Yeah, well, you was up front of me in the posse,

wasn't you. I never got a look nor a shot at him at all. This leg makes me a lousy posseman – same as it makes me a lousy everythin' else."

"Oh for God's sake ...!" Bill Cramer felt his own temper fraying out under the sun-smash. He forced it down again, like a good head deputy should. "You could try and brighten up some," he told his driver in a tone of strained reasonableness. "Seeing as it don't appear now as if we'll need to knock either you, or the rig, all over the Sansbois. If Kratoch kept on goin' round the edge there till he fell off, it won't be difficult to find what's left of him now. It could work out so we're back in Smith by sundown."

* * *

But it wasn't destined to be that convenient. The big grey's prints soon became childishly easy to read in the dusty chippings that lined most of the eastern edge of the mountains, apart from occasional hard outcrop. But the long even stretch between each set of them never seemed to shorten; which meant to tire. And although Paul Monkerud was forever bobbing up and down off his black to search for both horse and human blood, his sharp dark eyes never discovered a fleck of either.

"What did that shitbag bailiff feed it on – dynamite?" Marv Collins snarled disconsolately, at a point in the afternoon when the worst of the burn had gone out of the sun.

Marvin had been encouraging himself, since they started again, with some thoughts of spending a

night on The Row; if only they could pick up the
dead runaway and return in time for him to do that.
But now it was gone four o'clock and the long line of
mountains was starting to curl ominously leftward.

The three mounted deputies had by then pushed
on well ahead of Huttman and the toiling mule
team. The horsebackers knew only too well that not
far in front of them now was the military road that
slanted south-west from Fort Smith down to old
Fort Washita, past the Sansbois' northernmost
turrets.

Nowadays the road had decayed into a rough
wagon track. If Kratoch was really a dying man – or
by now a dead one – it would provide a handy route
for them back to Arkansas; but if he wasn't too far
gone, if he was somehow still in control of the
extraordinary saddle animal that he had been so
lucky to grab, then the old army route could have
taken him in the other direction: deep into the
Choctaw Plains, if he'd been able to keep going and
had had the wit to make use of it.

By now the lawman in Bill Cramer was fast
taking over from the downcast individual he
became when off duty. He had changed his opinion
that the hunky's horse was making the decisions up
ahead of them. It seemed to him now that although
the animal might have been running blind ahead of
the posse, at some point since then Kratoch had
snapped to and started to ride it.

That theory was confirmed beyond any doubt
when Cramer, in the lead, cut the old road. Reining
around and glancing down from the saddle, he

didn't need Monkerud pounding up behind him to explain the new situation they faced.

The big calked shoe-prints they'd been following had gone into the road at a right angle. Then they had scuffed sharply westward, before the marks faded to become mere scratches over the hard baked ruts of the present-day wagon track.

Paul Monkerud said in his brief way: "We'd best slow down now. We ain't about to take this smart hunky back with us today."

They rode ten more miles down the road into the blinding sundown, then bore off it for a further two miles to make camp on the banks of the barely flowing Brushy.

Marv Pollins, blaspheming steadily, then found himself told to help Huttman gather pulpwood from along the stream. As exercise went, it wasn't much like what he'd been planning on for this time of the evening. While he and the driver were doing that, Monkerud saw to the mules and Cramer put the horses on stake ropes.

After the long and unrewarded hours of pursuit under the fierce sun it became very trying for them to endure the lingering heat in the river bottom as dusk came on. All four of them were slumped down exhaustedly amongst a parched and yellowing growth of mullein and spearweed, while the Brushy trickled by like no more than a running tap; though still drawing a host of buzzing and biting insects to its snake-like course through the mud.

Pollins swiped at something that was nibbling under his left eye. That particular insect seemed to finally trigger his temper. A second later he spat a mouthful of coffee wrathfully into the small fire.

"Look here, Cramer, I don't say nothin' against this so-call drysalt meat and pan bread that Slim's fried up – but he's got no right to use this here gypwater for our fuckin' coffee!"

"I never used that water for it, nor wouldn't," Huttman told him angrily, motioning at the stagnant stream. "I topped up the can back at that mountain brook this mornin'. That's what I used, sonny. It's a shame if you don' like it."

Cramer lowered his irons to his plate, swallowing down a last piece of greasy hoecake. Tired though he was, he was made alert by the untypical sarcasm in Huttman's tone then.

The ex-cownurse was sitting in a stiff, awkward pose dictated by his leg injury. Cramer could picture how it must be for him: this heat to bear with plus a mess of shattered and still unhealed bone to torment him also.

He said distinctly: "Slim's doin' his best same as we all are." He paused and thought a moment, trying to find the right words to gentle them all down.

"Only think how Kratoch's feeling by this time … nothin' to eat at all most likely, and coughin' up bits of his lungs somewheres on the open prairie. With a horse that's bound to be ruined by now, even if that ain't showed yet to us who's comin' after."

The tense atmosphere between them did seem to ease after he said that, and he felt he'd done the trick of keeping the outfit amicable together. He relaxed, and must have dozed off for a while, then suddenly came to when he found Slim shaking his shoulder.

"You better wake up fast, Billy boy ..." the driver murmured urgently. "If I don't miss my guess Monk's gone off to fetch his little black book. Send that dirty-mouth kid off to his blankets or we'll have hell bustin' loose any moment."

Cramer shook off his tiredness with an effort. He saw that Marv Collins was still awake and by the fire, rocking back and forth moodily on his heels as he hunkered and gazed at the grey-red embers.

Cramer then glanced away upstream, and made out the vague tall shape of the zealot as he came striding back along the bottom from where they had put the wagon. You could tell it was Monkerud despite the dark, by the way his badge shone higher off the ground than it would on most deputies. And as he drew closer Cramer saw that he gripped something in one hand that was blacker than the darkness. Having ridden with him before he knew what it was apt to be without Huttman telling him.

He said: "Time to hit your bedroll, Marv. I want us to move out after the bohunk at first light."

But he could see by the look on Pollins's round features that what was coming wouldn't be headed off. A period of solitary contemplation didn't seem to have sweetened their junior member very much. He gave a contrary scowl through the dim firelight, grunting: "I'll go in a minute. I ain't so tired now. You needn' fret, I'll be ready enough tomorrow."

Cramer gave a fatalistic shrug as Paul Monkerud seated himself amongst his fellow lawmen. He opened the small book he had with him, doing that at random but with a certain formal deliberation. He began to read aloud from it, without intoning as a regular preacher might have done, but speaking in the ordinary conversational style that was approved of by the sect he had been raised in.

He began: "Genesis Thirteen, friends. Verses One to Three. *And Abram went up out of Egypt, he and his wife and all that he had, and Lot with him into the south. And Abram was –*"

"Looky here, spook, I sure-hell ain't takin' no Jesus talk from you after the kind of day I already done had! You wanna talk that shit you do it outen my hearin', unnerstand?"

Marvin Collins was up on his stocky legs, and glowering across at Monkerud like a young brush. bull. Monkerud continued in exactly the same fashion as before:

"*– was very rich in cattle, in silver, and in gold.*"

"Then he sure-hell wasn't a Goddam US deputy, this asshole wasn't!' Pollins bawled out at full lung. His eyes were starting to seem to pop loose from their surrounding round pudginess, shining crazily with exhaustion and rage. Cramer made to get up and go over to him, but Slim Huttman held him back and said in his ear:

"Aw, let it happen ... Let it happen a bit, anyway. It's about time this fuzzy-tailed hoodlum was lessoned. If Monk don't lesson him I know I shall, mebbe with lead. And you wouldn' like that no better than this, William."

Cramer chewed his lip, then gave a doubtful shrug and subsided again.

"And he went on his journeys from the south even to Bethel, unto the place where his tent had been at the beginning, between Bethel and Hai."

"I don' give a fart where this fuckin' tent got pitched at, spook! – hear me?"

Paul Monkerud shut the book in his hands and finally raised his dark eyes from it to look through the dying firelight. Some quality in them stopped the profane young lawman from adding to his blasphemies. Then Monkerud addressed him pleasantly enough: "Yes, Brother, I hear you." He gave a solemn nod and set the book aside.

He stood up, poker-thin and poker-straight, looming over the powerful young man with only the wisping fire between them. Pollins was breathing fast and hard, holding himself in defiant readiness to smash Monkerud in the stomach. But before that move could take place a couple of long stick-like arms took hold of Marvin Collins in a deceptive-looking grip that nevertheless rattled the air promptly out of his lungs.

"Hey, Cramer! Huttman! Git this damn spook off of me! Git –!"

But Marv ceased speaking from natural causes at that point. He had been effortlessly up-ended and held head down over the fire; in Comanche style except that he was not actually tied there.

He yelled and kicked and struggled, and tried to make a draw from that uncommon firing position, but Monkerud just held him with one hand then while he tossed his pistol from its holster with the other. He swung him gently to and fro above the hot ashes, ignoring his flailing arms. A few strands of his lank fair-ish hair began to hiss and form tight curls.

"Brother, you are cursed with a foul tongue," Monkerud observed with stern sympathy. "It is my bounden duty to aid you in your plight."

He lowered him a little, and Pollins's steady flow of oaths jumped up the scale to become a long crystal-like scream.

"Ah, my Brother! Now I begin to hear your true self ... Even yet we may save you from your Maker's Just Vengeance ... But fire, to truly purify, must perforce be intense."

He began to touch down his burden's head into the now differently-smelling ash. And that was when Bill Cramer's .45 hammer clinked back and the barrel was rammed in hard near Monkerud's lower vertebras.

"That's enough. Haul him up – *now*. Elsewise you get yours, Paul. Don't be dumb enough to think I wouldn't. Or that I wouldn't enjoy it."

Marv Pollins's conscientious saviour hesitated for a singeing, screeching further instant. Then he threw the young deputy aside like a sack of meal and picked up his Bible and walked away toward the tumbleweed without a backward glance.

*   *   *

Later in the night when Huttman had greased his burns with leaf fat, and he wasn't too uncomfortable, Marv Pollins muttered shakily from his bedroll: "Where does the ... spook get his ... his weird strength from, d'you reckon? I mean, I ain't no milk-fed veal exactly. And he's that thin and drawed out he don' look like he'd be nothin' at all to brace."

Slim smiled up at the starry sky. He'd taken note of those new awkward pauses in place of cuss words.

"It might be he has it straight from God, boy. I dassay he thinks that anyhow. You think a thing deep enough it's got a way of comin' true."

There was an uneasy silence while Marv addressed his mind to the alien subject of philosophy. Then he said with a kind of forlorn dignity: "I just might throw down on the ... on him for what he done to me tonight. I might at that."

"Sure you might," Slim agreed amiably.

"Well, I might too ... I mean, if it hadn' been for Bill buying in when he did I'd be like your ... right unsatisfyin' salt pork by now."

Slim had to chuckle, though he strove to make it sound friendly.

"Try and git some sleep now. And jes' don't ruff Monk's fur again unless he turns *real* religious on you nex' time. What you'd ought to keep in mind is Monk had already busted a man's neck when he was ten years younger than you are. But he ain't really so bad to be with save for the Bible punchin'. That's just a cross we all has to bear who rides with him." He paused, with another show of his teeth to the night sky, then added slyly: "Them *sonofabitch holy readin's*."

Pollins responded with a snort of grateful laughter, which carried to where Bill Cramer had thrown his own roll farther downstream.

Cramer hadn't heard the former exchange but that laugh told him the gist of it. Maybe the brief spell of pointless violence between the four of them had let off steam and done some good, he thought, as his mind began to float.

FIVE

Next morning at false dawn he stirred Slim up and got him slicing bacon on the wagon's tailgate. He and Monkerud between them did most of the boy's chores, for his head was a rich scarlet under the hair that was left on and as swollen as a mush-melon. He bellowed like a de-calfed wet cow when the zealot came ghosting up behind him and helped him on suddenly with his hat, as a sort of dour reminder. Not that Deputy Pollins looked as if he needed any reminding.

After they broke camp they headed back to the wagon road and continued to follow it south-west through the usually lush, now brown Prairie Plains. After fifteen more uneventful miles had gone by Paul Monkerud came reining up beside Cramer, his long thin face covered with tiny globules of moisture and looking baffled.

The normally taciturn zealot said: "Look, this ain't makin' any kind of sense. Neither the hunky nor his horse have got any business to be alive, leave out still on the run in this heat. I don' believe he's got bad lungs, whatever them fool medics said. Only think of the way he jumped on the Judge at the start of all this. He ain't acted all along like a lunger could of."

Cramer pulled his dun back to a more conversational gait. "What you said then about the heat could have a bearin' on it," he mumbled through his chewing plug.

"What?"

"Sorry ... Was sayin' that this heat could be a part of the mystery. I've a cousin who had to go and live far west for his lungs. Well, this year the far west has come to the Choctaw Nation. It came to me that maybe Kratoch's done some benefitin' from it."

Monkerud considered that as they loped along together, with Pollins riding aloofly far back near the bouncing tumbleweed. "Nope," he grunted finally in his definite way. "I kin read the sign of a Greater Hand in this than a freak of climate. It could be that hunky is *meant* to run free," he concluded solemnly.

Bill Cramer jerked his head sideways with an ugly scowl.

"Ain't even you had enough of that line of thinkin' lately? There's Marv back there with a half-roasted skull because you just couldn't curb yourself down, could you ... I don't want to hear another word about Kratoch havin' a *greater hand* to deal for him. You got that clear?"

"As glass lights, friend," Monkerud said in the superior, forgiving tone that was almost as annoying sometimes as his sermonizing.

Partly to change the subject Cramer asked: 'You plumb certain he ain't forked off this track somewheres?"

The lawman in Paul Monkerud promptly displaced the fanatic side of his divided nature. "Nah, he ain't forked off it. I keep findin' things. We'se still runnin' him."

They found positive proof of that statement as that second day out of blistering heat turned gradually into golden evening. It was Slim who spotted the slight break in the stem-curing grass beside the beaten track, from his position above the horsebackers on the wagon seat.

"Hey, Marv! Go see what's made that hole there ..."

It was a dead wild turkey. Which wasn't all that odd a discovery in a summer which was dropping scores of wild creatures lifeless all over the Southwest. But this turkey hen had not expired from the heat but from heavy buckshot, and subsequently it had lost its breast flesh and legs. Beside the shredded and half-plucked remains was an extra-scorched bit of prairie where Julius Kratoch had hastily cooked his first meal since leaving Arkansas.

"Well, now," Bill Cramer said bleakly after he had ridden back to take a look. "What we got us now is one *nourished* hunky to chase after. When you think how well he was doin' before I guess he's a blame fireball with that inside him."

All four of them felt very jaded and depressed. While they were still standing around the abandoned turkey feast, an Indian family showed themselves against the prairieline to the south-west, heading up along the old road like a walking section of picket fence.

Marv Pollins said naively: "Mebbe them redsticks seed him go by earlier on and could tell us."

"Gwan!" Huttman mocked him as he climbed wearily back on the wagon. "Choctaws never see anything of whites' business, any more than the proper wild 'uns do over on the Sill reservation. That's one thing they all got in common – not seein' what don't concern them."

"Yeh, that's true," Cramer murmured, shading his eyes to watch the family's filing progress. His attention sharpened a little. "... On the other hand they ain't usually apt to leave a road in their own country just to miss saying hello."

The other three gazed again in that direction. They also now saw that the short line of slender brown forms, a shade darker than the backcloth of withered grass, had now angled northward off the trail on a new course that would take them clear of the government men.

Monkerud said thinly: "Yep, they seen something all right. I'll get my carbine out of the rig." He toed up on to his black and wheeled toward the wagon through the crackling tall grass.

"Marv, better pull yours out too. And Slim – has that thing up there with you got at least somethin' in the breech? We'll close up around you as we ride now: I know it seems ridiculous all for this poor bohunk, but I don't aim to let him pull off the kind of surprise that turkey had."

It did feel ridiculous to be travelling in the sort of close formation that would have suited a laden

Army pay-wagon rather than the present case of an empty Studebaker tumbleweed. But they each felt they were approaching the end of this now, and those big Double-O's in the turkey carcass had imbued them with caution.

But five more miles went past and they had left the long swell in the prairie which the Indian family had come from. Nothing ... The ground was dipping down now. Ahead toward the skyline was a straggling line of scrub oaks and cottonwood, along one of the nameless creeks that fed northward into the Canadian. The sun was now sitting so close to the rim of the earth that is seemed to flash and dazzle directly behind the creek timber.

Then they saw it: the bailiff's horse, lying twenty yards or so from the wagon road, so that it had gone down precisely due west. No sign of the hunky – unless he had fallen right behind it. But when they drew closer they could see he wasn't anywhere by the animal.

Bill Cramer let out his breath and spurred forward, half-hooding his eyes to squint over the grey's shimmering flanks. It seemed that the indestructible whisky maker had kept going on foot once the grey foundered. But he couldn't have got far in the heat, and Cramer felt a sudden wild urge to run him down and end it. As the dun stretched out beneath him he heard one, or both, of the other two who were a-saddle come drumming after him, and Slim's yells in the rear as he whaled the mules to keep up.

Cramer did see the trap – but not before it was sprung. As he sped forward his mind began to sort of tick off warning signs one by one, in a state of rising panic that still stopped numbly short of reaction.

... The motionless horse, right in the path of the sun, funny really ... The long scatter of trees behind it, not as long a piece as he'd figured, really quite close, their actual position distorted by that damned sun-glare striking through the glossy leaves ...

And then the hunky. Bolting out of the trees at an incredible lick from where they grew thinnest – and where the great Christmas orange right behind him limned his plunging outline with an edge of red flame ...

Belatedly he grasped it all and tried to pull up; but the dun was really travelling and all he could effect was a bone-jarring swerve. The air seemed to suck at him and he felt himself dumping off, clawing his saddlegun by instinct from the boot as he went. He heard his voice yelling: *"Back! Back, Godammit!"*

And then he hit down and rolled and started shooting. From the tail of his eye he saw Monkerud shooting from the rearing black, a little ways over on his left.

But he knew, as Paul must have been knowing also that same second, that it was no damned good ... Not shooting straight into the sun the way Kratoch had rigged it. That shotgun he was *still not using* would have been no more of a danger than a boy's toy weapon to the pair of them with rifles – if they could have seen him. With no choke left on it, with sawn-off barrels, it was no good to him outside twenty yards. But the bastard had known that and planned for it.

That deadly blindness wasn't quite absolute though very nearly: the shotgun itself was only a shimmer within the glare, yet he got a clear impression of its beaded sight tilting up at last; and of Kratoch's berserk face over the sight. Though he still couldn't see *him* ... He was not merely blinded by the sun, he was disorientated by it as well.

He kept on doggedly, helplessly firing in the direction where he couldn't see. The metal of the lever, warm before he fired the first shell, was now burning his skin as if he'd been using it all day as he jacked up replacements. It was an odd thing to be aware of at that moment.

The shotgun finally exploded as the hunky came staggering within its range. Shot ripped into a huge chunk of prairie as if from a rain cloud. A Double-O prodded under his left boot like a bullet, making him kick that leg up behind him in a nervous spasm as if he was doing some mad horizontal exercise. He tried to keep firing, but the mighty blast at close quarters seemed to have paralysed his brain clear down to his hands.

The shotgun bellowed with its other barrel, and he heard Monkerud's black make the distinctive cry of a mortally struck horse; then some more stubborn snaps from Paul's carbine – sounding as over-quick and useless as ever. He realized despondingly that Paul wasn't far enough way from him to be out of the sun line. Kratoch still had them both helpless if he just stayed where he was and made a fast reload.

Vaguely, now, he heard the tumbleweed grinding and lurching over the hard uneven sod. It came to him that he'd had no room in his head lately for the tumbleweed and the other two in their team. Then Slim's voice was hollering: "*Kratoch*! Drop it down, mister ... Us two ain't lookin in the sun and we both got rifles. To be percise we got you in a good enough crossfire, me up here and our fourth man behind the endgate. That Greener won't reach to us e'en halfway. But we're sure fixin' to kill you if you try and find that out."

Julius Kratoch had now broken the gun and pushed in more loads and snapped it back in line. He turned his head very slightly away from the piece of business he already had in hand. All he could see on the wagon that might interfere with that business was what looked to him like a long-barrelled old Winchester '63. And it was being held on him by what looked like a common cowhand rather than a government marshal.

He licked his taut lips, wondering about it. That was when Marv Pollins's modern rifle briefly jetted fire from near the tailgate and a round passed discouragingly close to the end of his nose. Almost together with it, Huttman's ancient repeater did something similar near the backs of his ears.

Kratoch gave a foreign-sounding exclamation of pent-up rage and despair. Then there was a muffled rattle as what had so nearly been a death machine fell into the grass. Followed by a softer noise as the hunky dropped down beside it.

* * *

The first thing that Bill Cramer felt, when he could feel again, was deep and abiding shame.

He was the one who was supposed to be in charge of this expedition, as one of Judge Parker's formerly most esteemed deputies and one who was still reckoned to be sound enough apart from honing for his absent wife. Yet he had let himself be outsmarted by a consumptive bootlegger on a borrowed horse and toting a short-range shotgun. Damned nearly killed by him, too ...

Anger, in place of sunlight, now made him blind when he went over to where Julius Kratoch lay panting. He gave him a vicious jab with the still smoking saddlegun, seeing him still through a retained jumble of dancing red rings.

"On your feet ... You ain't about to fool me the way you fooled 'em in court. Get up and march to the wagon – *go on, march!*"

Oddly enough it was the stone-faced (and almost as mortified) Paul Monkerud who now took him on one side and lectured him in a low voice.

"Slack off, Bill. The hunky's done up, genuine done up. Only think of all he's gone through since he first hightailed. Only listen to him, come to that."

Cramer swung impatiently away from him. But he had no choice but to listen to the curious sounds that were coming from Kratoch's heaving ribcage.

The final effort of sprinting from the trees had turned his sickly breathing into a steam calliope that couldn't be shut off. Whatever ailed his lungs was evidently retarding his recovery from the undue exertion and turning his features blue and twisted with distress.

Pollins and Huttman had walked over by then, and he found it a sight easier to bark an order than to say what he knew he should to them.

"OK, pick him up and carry him to the rig. And you'd best take that tick quilt from underneath for him to lie on in the box. Mind you lock him in tight. But don't put him in shackes yet," he added grudgingly.

Slim eyed him with shrewd understanding as he stooped down to take hold of Kratoch's bony shoulders. Marv Pollins looked just once at Monkerud before he attended to the prisoner's feet end; but that single penetrating stare from the red-scalped young lawman was enough to fetch a trace of color to the zealot's own greyish skin. Marv grinned, rubbing in the salt with typical youthful exuberance as he moved off with his half of the burden.

"Stand aside, spook ... This here is tricky work as needs doin' without any dumb fuckin' mistakes," he emphasized with considerable satisfaction.

When they had Kratoch locked safely in the wagon cage, and lying fairly comfortably on the shuck mattress, he and Huttman took the mules and the tumbleweed on to the creek from which they'd been ambushed, while the other pair checked the horses that had been involved in the gun battle.

There was still a dab of life in Monkerud's black. He took out his revolver and put it behind its ear, murmuring: "Just as well we brung that spare along." But he didn't look as laconic as he sounded over losing his personal horse, as Cramer noticed. He'd known before now that horseflesh brought out what passed for a soft spot in Monkerud.

They moved on to inspect the dun, which had now settled down from its fright and was plucking hungrily at a green fringe of grass which grew around a spillage of bog from the creek.

"The tough way you lit down then you'd think he'd like to bust himself up," Monkerud remarked as Cramer felt of the dun's still trembling legs.

"Yeh, that was lucky. The whole dadrotted mess weren't exactly unlucky. That's what galls," Cramer said bitterly.

Monkerud nodded and grunted in accord. "You and me both was acting like green kids in that fight, Bill. And our necks got saved by one sensible-acting kid in the right place and a stove-up driver ... As you say, it galls some."

After looking to their own animals they went back to make sure that Kratoch's hardy and long-suffering mount was as dead as it seemed. It was, and had been for some hours past. A gush of blood had congealed on the bit chain and in the grass there. Bill Cramer gave an insuck of breath which expressed his distaste and reluctant admiration, mixed up together.

"You got to hand it to that wreck of a bohunk. He rode that thing to death judgin' it perfect as any

Commanch'. Then made sure it went down near enough the crick bank and also in the way of the sun."

Paul Monkerud corrected him, stirring the stiff grey absently with a foot. "No, it was clever'n even that. He had to put it down where he *guessed the sun might be* around the time we showed up. 'Cause without we fogged in like idiots plumb on that baited line, then his whole notion of comin' at us straight out of the sun wasn't going to work."

Bill Cramer thought about that. He said slowly: "If he's as sharp as that ... it seems funny he would just run any which way. I mean, he could of pulled that sun dance on us back near the hills just as well ... could of shot the horse by some trees where he wanted it last evening, and with less doubt about it. The sun was there just the same. What day ain't it this year ..."

The zealot narrowed his black eyes as they flickered off toward the south. "You thinkin' what I am now, Bill? That this ain't so far from the Cross Timbers?"

"Yeh, I was. But it don't make much sense to. Kratoch don't ride with the class of outlaw you get in the Cross Timbers. They'd scramble a juice runner for breakfast and have his boudins for supper."

Monkerud shrugged. "That's true. I guess he was just running away from us." But he still looked southward in a dissatisfied way.

"I know one thing: whether he's sick or healthy I'm keepin' one of our sets of eyes jammed open on that hunky clear back to Smith. On him and him alone. Day and night. That way we won't get no more trouble even with him."

That straightforward intention was one which he was to recall somewhat ruefully in the days that lay ahead.

SIX

When they rejoined the others they saw that the now occupied prison wagon had been left in a careless fashion, half-tipped down into the gully of the creek, brought to a halt there at a lurching angle by a jagged-ended trunk of salt cedar.

Marv Pollins, whistling cheerily, was digging a firepit closer to the thread of muddy water. Huttman was just about to unhitch the wheel team of mules as the last rays of the treacherous sun struck fire from their harness. The leaders were already unhitched, and the saddlestock munching oats on their picket ropes.

Bill Cramer still found it easier to be snippy than amicable.

"Slim – you should know better than to leave the rig up in the air that way. Get it shifted. That bole it's bumped on will do to chain the hunky to in a moment. Then you can try to cook somethin' better for us than you done so far this trip," he finished dryly.

Slim, with his face mournfully impassive, left the wheelers still hitched and climbed wearily back on the seat. "*Whoa-up* ... haunch back, you bug-gers ..."

The tumbleweed stuck in its awkward position for another few seconds, then began to inch backward. Julius Kratoch watched the manoeuvre bright-eyed from his lying position in the box, propped on one elbow. His eyes were peculiarly bright, which was presumably a sign of his illness. On the other hand it certainly went just as well with his intelligence. Bill Cramer's mind was very open on that point after what had happened in the last hour.

Finally the wagon tipped back to the horizontal once more and Slim then managed to haul the mules left of the obstacle so they could move on down the bank. He parked it on a piece of flat and jumped down to drag a length of log chain from underneath it, together with a set of shackles.

Kratoch had recovered a bit by then. He stood up quite sturdily and held his arms out for the shackles, then dropped down to the ground and meekly allowed himself to be herded over to the thick cedar stump and chained to it.

Slim then made use of the lowered tailgate to prepare 'something better' for their supper, as instructed. He found his sourdough keg and peered doubtfully inside, grumbling to no-one in par-ticular: "This don' look so promisin'. Cain't hardly expect it to, after jouncin' it fit to blow up. Still, we'll see ..."

Pollins had a good fire going by then. Slim tipped a soft mass of sourdough onto a board and made an attempt to rough-chunk it into some sort of recognizable shapes. Then he greased the biscuits-to-be and put them in a pan and took it over to the fire to prop on the logs.

He returned to the tailgate and was soon cramming half a dozen thick steaks into a skillet, limping back to the blaze with that and an iron spider. He set them in place with a flourish and told Marv to flip the steaks over when they looked ready for it. He figured that he'd done maybe about enough now, but was then struck by a culinary after-thought: that pot of beans he'd had soaking ever since they broke the last camp. He brought them out and shoved them on to boil.

Lastly – and with an air of greater certainty than hitherto – he spooned a large amount of Triple X into a vast cow-camp coffeepot which had been with him from before he took to law-dogging. He half-filled it with water and hung it by a trammel hook from a crane of cottonwood boughs which Pollins had been rigging in the meantime.

The total result was unquestionably Slim Huttman's most major endeavour at trailside chefdom; though perhaps it couldn't be called a total success. The biscuits tilted over on the logs and half the contents ran out before hardening had taken effect. The other half came out later with the consistency of hammered steel. Next to that the frijoles were merely like quite soft bullets, bloodied with tomato and primed with chilies.

But the steaks weren't too bad, and the other lawmen felt on the whole fairly benevolent toward the mature novice who had turned them out; though they were undoubtedly influenced in their benevolence by the thought that they would only be sampling a couple more such repasts now that they'd got Kratoch back.

The hunky ate his portion in silence except for a steady racking cough. He hadn't said above six words since he was retaken. He sat cross-legged against the stump with the tin plate wedged expertly between his knees. He managed his eating tools in a nonchalant way too, despite being shackled. .

As the four of them consumed their own grub Pollins said: "It's plain that one's no stranger to being shackled in his line of business. How many times he been up for it to the old judge? Two-three times?"

"More than that. Kratoch's an old hand," Cramer grunted as he cut off a corner of Battle Axe with his knife. He popped it in his scarred cheek and grinned faintly for the first time that day. "Which ain't to say he shinned up him before this time. I shouldn't wonder if Isaac don't hand him ten years for that damn cheek – and for when he gits to learn of our gunnin' bee that finished it."

Although he'd said that last bit lightly, it was still rather too close to the reality of those scary moments facing the sun and the shotgun for their answering grins to have much substance.

The proud cook had been twisting himself a brown cigarette, and he now tossed the makings over to Pollins who was out of them. The hunky then startled them by asking for a smoke too; they had just naturally assumed that with his lungs he wouldn't. Pollins rolled him one after his own and took it over and stuck it in his mouth. He lit it for him from a waterproof matchbox Kratoch had in his pocket.

Then Paul Monkerud got suddenly and silently to his lank height and left the fire.

"Uh-uh, here it comes ..." Slim said warningly between puffs. "Now jes' see you don't climb his hump like yestiddy, boy. You made your point backalong that he made a fine ol' –" Slim caught Cramer's flinty stare and decided to put it another way. "– that he was mebbe a mite out of luck today. But let him play at bein' Jehovah if he wants to without havin' you cuss him out every verse."

"Screw him, why shouldn' I – sin-busting sonofabitch. This head a mine still hurts like I been counted coup on by a passel of Kiowas," Marv complained with ominous spirit and pugnacity.

But as those words themselves showed, the harsh treatment he had received the night before was still influencing him deeply. When the zealot came back and recited his usual three random verses – from *Joshua* this time – he restrained his comments to a face-saving subtone that Monkerud seemed to overlook; perhaps because the offending heathen concerned had probably saved his own life a short while ago.

True to his word, Cramer split the coming night into four watches so that Julius Kratoch would never be unobserved at any point. He chose to take the first watch himself, to be followed by Pollins and Monkerud in that order. Huttman was to take the watch on through to daytime again.

It wasn't a popular idea with any of them. Cramer felt himself that it did seem a foolish precaution to be taking over one sick and exhausted prisoner, who could hardly do much now even if he had proved that he packed an ingenious set of brains. But Cramer had also reminded himself that a good lawman rarely got into trouble through taking too few chances; while there were federal bodies planted all over the Territory whose owners had taken just one too many.

He knew there were always some misguided gents in the Nations who would see it as a plain and natural duty to try to release any government prisoner they came across. He had already made enough bad mistakes for one day, and surely didn't plan to make any more.

As it happened they did get some unexpected visitors before the night was out.

* * *

Slim Huttman had been concerned to find the fire sunk so low when Monkerud came and shook him awake to take over the guard.

Once he had ridden a circle around the camp and checked that the prisoner was sleeping safe and sound in the tumbleweed, Slim began collecting brush from along the creek and feeding it to the thin wisp of smoke.

He didn't blame Monkerud for that piece of negligence; the swelter of daytime heat hung on through most of the darkness now as this extraordinary summer continued, and the first three on graveyard shift had had little need of extra warmth. There was enough heat in the fire to keep the big coffeepot going, which was all they had cared about. Slim wouldn't have cared about it any more than that himself, but for his new line of employment.

... He sure as hell didn't plan to make breakfast on a cold open stove. He reckoned that after his top performance last evening the boys would expect something better from him than that.

Small flames began to pick up again under the heap of tinder-dry brush. He hunkered beside it, holding his hands out, wondering why it had been that he had taken so over-long in his life to discover his natural talent for biscuit-shooting.

Why, then he thought of all the incompetent characters he'd known who'd like to poisoned their outfits – formerly along big cattle trails like the Western and the Pecos, and more lately in various small-sized federal operations like this present job he was on – he was sheerly astounded that nobody had ever found out there was a natural born cookie in their midst who could have beat the regular pothooks to flinders ...

He must have sleepily brooded on that mystery for some time; though every so often he straightened up to pour more coffee into his cup and sink down again to drink it. The last time he

made that effort he noticed vaguely than a smear of
false dawn now lay over the area of prairie they had
come from.

Then, with shocking suddenness, a deep, clipped
sort of voice called from close by: "Hello the fire!"

In actual fact, Slim's instincts as a nighthawk
were distinctly more developed than were his
budding culinary skills. That voice was still
speaking when he grabbed his saddlegun, after a
long diving plunge across the ground to where he'd
left it propped. In the next second after that he had
arced the long barrel eastward toward the sound
and was slammed down behind it, with his trigger
finger trembling to let off the shot that was already
chambered. He didn't attempt to use the sight in
this half-dark; if anything showed he would simply
snap-shoot. He knew he was quite good at that.

The sausage-like shape of Marvin Pollins
suddenly reared up from where he was lying over on
the wagon's far side. "*Whatinhell was that?*"

Then Bill Cramer roared from the rig's near side:
"*Roll out! We got company!*"

There followed a turmoil of movement and
shouting as the three off-duty lawmen blundered
instinctively toward the cage end of the prison
wagon, jerking their sixes from their holsters as
they formed a protective triangle there. Cramer
bawled again: "*Where's that Goddam Slim at?*"

Paul Monkerud said to him quietly: "He's right
where he ought to be, lookin' at you over that old
pipe a his from by the fire."

"Oh ..."

There followed a short silence except for a tense clinking back of hammers. Then the same deep voice as before spoke again, this time with a faint note of amusement in it.

"Marshals, there's no call to act so jumpy. We're lawmen too ... We wouldn't have exactly hailed you if we'd had mischief in mind. Permission to come in, please?"

It was the accent, more than the reassuring words themselves, which made Bill Cramer stuff his handgun away in some embarrassment. Mission school English ...

"All right, come in," he growled, by no means reconciled to even a friendly visit at this time.

Three Choctaw Lighthorse policemen were outlined briefly over the lip of the easterly bank. They slid on down to them, their big showy revolvers jouncing against their hips. A horse whickered from behind them, from where they'd evidently tied their mounts.

The one in the middle, the previous speaker, now said: "Sorry we disturbed you. But it was urgent we found you without delay."

"You been lookin' for us?" Bill Cramer asked harshly. "How come?"

The tall middle Choctaw, who was evidently the head man of the trio, took a careful long stare to make sure he was addressing his equal in the white team. He gestured over his shoulder toward the now true-dawning east. "Back on the trail you passed some of our people, remember?"

Cramer nodded. The Indian family who'd seen

Kratoch laying for them, most likely, and who had then typically sheered off to stay out of it.

"I remember," he grated coldly. "It still don't answer my question why you came pokin' around to find us. We're on federal business, takin' a white prisoner back to Smith. There's no reason for you to butt in."

The Choctaw gave a patient sigh. "No, of course not. It's a longish story, Marshal, and we've been travelling a ways to get here. Would you have such a thing as a cup of coffee before I tell you about it?"

Cramer led them unwillingly over to the fire. Slim was now rifleless once more and stirring the blaze to greater life. The flames glistened on the Indians' short and combed-back white style hair.

But they sat down cross-legged like any other tribesmen, and their boss began to talk as soon as his throat was warmed and wetted.

'I'll start at the beginning. Me and my two partners were riding up beside the Katy line around this time yesterday, north of McAlester. There had been a report of some trouble in one of those railroad shanty towns the trackmen left behind. Well, the trouble turned out to be nothing much, and we handled it and were heading back down the tracks again when we found this woman." He paused, then said with a stress: "This white woman." He paused again. "Not that we realized that for some while."

"You mean 'cause it was shit-dark at the time, John, same as it still is now?" Marv Pollins put in intelligently. Cramer motioned him to keep quiet.

The mention of a white woman was beginning to clarify why the Lighthorse party had wanted to contact some federal law.

"No, not for that reason, Marshal," the Choctaw answered Pollins, with a wry look crossing his rather fine features. "But I'll get to that in a moment. The woman had been left just by the tracks, not far from McAlester. She was – she was in very poor shape after being, uh, assaulted by a bunch of other females whose identity we have not been able to establish so far."

Cramer's experienced gaze fastened on the Choctaw's. "By that you mean they were Indian women, no doubt," he grunted with a touch of sarcasm.

"As I said that has not been established," the policeman said blandly.

"Nor ain't apt to be neither ... Look, I still can't figger how you came to be lookin' for *us*. We ain't been nowhere near the Katy railroad this trip."

Another of the Choctaws spoke up for the first time. "It's this way, Marshal: the family you passed spoke of seeing you to others of our people – and so on. News travels fast by such means in the Nation. We heard where you were not long after we had picked the poor woman up. We then headed this way because yours is the nearest to us of Judge Parker's travelling outfits, as far as we knew."

Cramer nodded. The story might well be straight. There was nothing yet invented that was as fast as a backtrail telegraph.

"What had she been up to, this woman?" he asked curiously.

"Singing," the head Choctaw told him deadpan.

"What?"

"Singing. She was – I guess I should still say she is – a professional singer. It seems she had come down from Saint Louis to give a performance for some of those dagos who work our mines around McAlester," the Indian murmured with a distinct lack of enthusiasm.

"Huh. She a dago too?"

"I really wouldn't know, Marshal." He gave a curious half-smile. "It's a thing you'll have to judge for yourself."

Cramer bristled at the 'have to' part. "You're way ahead of me, mister. If it's in your head that I can be whipsawed to take this woman off your hands, you better think again."

The Indian looked puzzled. From where he squatted he could see into the almost empty prison wagon, where Julius Kratoch had been wide awake since their arrival and was still staring down at them all. He brought his black eyes back to Cramer and said reasonably: "Why not? I see you've got nothing like a full load on."

"Ah, that may be ... but Judge Parker has sent us out on a special assignment. That bird you see there in the cage has to go to Arkansas on his lonesome, with no other men to go back with."

He realized even as he was saying that what this smooth-talking buck's answer was liable to be.

"But this wouldn't be another man, Marshal. Like I say, this is a female we want shed of."

SEVEN

Cramer and his fellow deputies eyed each other askance.

Marv Pollins was flashing a ribald grin at the notion. Slim Huttman was looking very wary of it indeed. And thunderheads of scandalized wrath were building in the zealot's expression.

Cramer swung back to face the Indian. "Sorry, mister, but it ain't to be thought of. Dammit – we got a man in there. A sick man, too."

He scowled impatiently at the unchanging dark visage. "Look, John, mebbe you can't see it the same as us fellers, but it just wouldn't be fittin' for them to ride back together in the one cage. I see your problem: but you'll have to find some other way to get her to Fort Smith, if that's what you're bound and determined on. I must say it don't seem the right answer to me anyway. I mean, what crime is she supposed to of done, save for gettin' crosswise of your own women some way you ain't explained yet?" he asked him curtly. It seemed to him that there still plenty under the dust here.

The head Choctaw spread out his hands in a

manner that was frank and evasive both together.

"It's true she has committed no crime, Marshal. On the face of it she could be shipped straight back where she came from. But when you take a look at her I doubt you'll favor that way of handling it any more than we did."

This Quaker-schooled Light Horsemen was one very bland Indian; but again he had that ghost of a grin on his lips when he said that last bit. Cramer poked his head at him suspiciously.

"Where's she at now?"

"Back with the horses. Come, I'll introduce you to her."

The four deputies uneasily followed the red policemen up the bank and over the nearby piece of prairie. There was now a bunch of ponies pegged there, three of them with the saddles cinched rather forward of where a cowhand would have placed them. The fourth mount, a splash white, trailed a lead rope from the harness. That one had been rigged with a firm double cinch in the usual position, and bore a sagging burden that was still oddly dark all over to look at in the now brightening morning. It was also, somehow, birdlike. The woman was for all the world like a dark and shapeless great bird as she slumped there motionless in the saddle.

Then they came a bit closer; and even the tight-lipped Monkerud was moved to make a shaken comment by the woman on the skewbald pony.

"Dear Jesus," he mumbled unsteadily (which

mild enough phrase told his partners following behind him how disturbed the rigid non-blasphemer
really was) "– someone's tar-and-feathered her ..."

* * *

There was a long moment of gaping incredulity. Then
Bill Cramer suddenly wheeled on the head Indian
and grabbed his jacket front in a squeezing vise.

"Now see here, John," he told him softly, "you'd
be right smart to give us this whole tale ... and not
just the bits you calkilate will go down smoothest
with us ..." He gave him a little shake to emphasize
that point, then abruptly set him loose.

The Choctaw licked his lips. His two companions
had edged in to side him; but he was mindful that
there were only two of them. He didn't fancy his
outfit's chances of bucking this scar-faced deputy
who'd threatened him. Or the tall thin one with the
mad eyes, for that matter. Or the dozy-looking one
who looked like a broken-down cowhand, but who
didn't act dozy in the least when he was going for his
rifle. Even the young one with the curious burned
scalp didn't exactly fill him with eagerness to pull
his big revolver on him. And when he thought of the
great and far-reaching power of the Hanging Judge
behind all four of them, he was definitely inclined to
accept the suggestion that it was time all cards were
turned over.

"All right, Marshal, it was as you figured. She
went and upset some of our Choctaw girls. It was
really her own fault – and I'm not just saying that the

way you'd expect me to. You see, she was only engaged to entertain the miners, but she had some foolishness in her mind that she shouldn't quit the Territory without giving the local folks a chance to hear her voice."

The Indian broke off his account to make a slight grimace of incomprehension. "She's kind of conceited about her voice, so we understood. Not that she's used it to us but to cry and moan with, ever since we found her. And over the last few miles here she hasn't made any sound at all."

"That ain't hardly a wonder after what was done to her," Cramer grated back. "Get on with it."

"Yes, well, after she gave her last show for the dagos it seems she went pokin' around McAlester to find some place where she could give the locals a musical treat of a lifetime. She wound up at a church social."

"She got tar-and-feathered at a *church social*? Mister, I hope you ain't guyin' me."

The Indian raised his hands defensively. "It was after the social that the trouble started. It seems Madam Deduras – that's her name, Madam Deduras, she goes around calling herself a madam in public, don't ask me why, Marshal – well, as I was saying, it seems Madam Deduras here was a big success at this social. But strictly with the menfolks, if you take my meaning."

The four lawmen switched their eyes off the Choctaws to stare hypnotically again at the mute woman on the pony. Slim Huttman murmured: "Did I hear you rightly then, John? *This here* went down well with your men?"

"One thing's for sure: this shit about her havin' a purty voice has got to be true shit," Marv Collins declared with a braying guffaw.

The Indian sighed. "You-all ought to remember it happened before she got to look the way she does. From what I heard she ain't a bad-looking woman in herself. You can still see well enough that the size of her is – unusual."

They all took another inspection of the silent Madam Deduras. She was a big woman, it was true; and big in several wrong places as well as in the right places. But Bill Cramer had caught the odd note in the Choctaw's tone when he'd spoken just then of her size. He was remembering that Indians generally didn't look on a big fat woman in the same critical light as most Caucasians did. They tended to react quite differently.

Cramer began dimly to imagine how a fat, conceited, citified, plumb ignorant woman singer might have misunderstood the reason for her popularity with male Choctaw Indians. And how, later on, a bunch of smaller-sized and evilly-jealous squaws might have caught her in some downtrack gully in McAlester with their tar bucket and sack of chicken feathers.

He said slowly: "Give us a moment alone, John, uh?" He beckoned the other three to follow him away from the now much more optimistic Light Horsemen.

"I forbid it. *I absolutely forbid it*!" Paul Monkerud thundered before Cramer had managed to utter a word to them in private.

"You forbid what?" he countered mildly.

"Why, to take her along, of course! It would be an outrage in the sight of our Almighty Father!"

"You figger He would be best pleased if we just forget about her, that so? Just leave her tar-and-feathered with them bucks ..."

The zealot flushed up and looked stubbornly confused. "Well, no, but –"

"Look, there's the chain bar in the tumbleweed," Slim said in a conciliatory way. "We could ride 'em back together, but chained apart. That way'd be decent whatever else."

Marv's coarse merriment rang out again over the prairie. "You'd fix to chain the hunky away from *her*?" He jabbed a thumb at the mute blackened figure. "You'd chain a shadder of a man away from she who ain't a woman at all that I kin see ..." He shook his red-ringed head in amazement. "I'd allow even Monk can't be really sniffin' poontang in that situation."

"That's not the point, Pollins," Monkerud said patiently.

"So what is the ... the doggone point? Tell me."

"They ain't man and wife. That's the whole of the point. You don't put a man and a woman in one rig without they're wedded."

The zealot's mouth closed like a baitpan trap and his eyes looked through them all in the insufferable way they often did.

Cramer took a step toward him. "Now you hear this, Paul. You ain't the one in charge of this run. I am. What Marv says makes plain enough sense to me. The notion of either of them two cozyin' up is pure dee madness to anyone 'cept to you. More than ever when you think they'll only be in the blame rig together for a day or so."

He paused, looking at that bitter closed face and feeling the mind behind it just the same. He pitched his voice more firmly. "I don't go round aimin' to teach you how to be Christian, like you try and do to us every suppertime we're stuck with you. But this is *my way* of being so. You think what you like about it. But the woman goes in the rig with Kratoch. And with no chaining apart less'n they's, uh, violent together. And that's final."

Paul Monkerud looked as if several fuses were burning out inside him to center on a massive charge of dynamite. But all he said was: "Then on your head be it, Brother. On your head be it."

Cramer led them back to the Lighthorse party.

"Right, we'll take her on with us the way you want." He glanced sideways with a wince of distaste. "I must say, mister, it would of been a kindly act if you'd tried to scrape some of that off her before she rode."

The head Indian gave an apologetic shrug. "I know. But there wasn't enough time for that if we were to catch up with you by now. That seemed more important." He gave another ironical grin. "Us buck police are a bit skittish of cleanin' up a white woman, as maybe you'll understand. By the way, there's some traps of hers we brought along with us. Nothing much, just a bag with some travelling plunder inside." He waved an arm and one of the other pair fetched a new-looking cowhide valise from behind his saddle and dumped it on the grass. "She's got some money in that too, Marshal – and it's all still there," the head Light Horseman added pointedly.

After that there didn't seem much more to be said between the two groups of lawmen. Slim Huttman braced himself and went over to help the woman down off the pony. She gave a mighty start when he touched her arm, looking down at him as if he were an awning post that had suddenly turned human. Then she gave a loud sobbing cry and slid down heavily where he was waiting to hold her.

Marv Pollins called over: "Blamed if she ain't shinin' up to you already, Slimmy!"

His facetious laugh rolled over the prairie as the three Indians rode away.

EIGHT

Bill Cramer squared his shoulders and walked resolutely up to the woman.

"Howdy, ma'am. Sure am sorry to see you the way you are. There's no accounting for Injuns and never will be, I reckon. But we'll soon have you cleaned up. Then we'll take you on with us to Fort Smith. That's close by in Arkansas, Miss Deduras," he added kindly when he saw there was no understanding on her daubed and darkened face. "They'll see about gettin' you back east again once we're in Smith."

She suddenly jerked up her head at him. "What you call me ... is not my name," she said in a surprisingly strong tone of voice.

Cramer rubbed his mouth uneasily. "The Lighthorse – I mean the Injuns, ma'am – they said you was called Deduras." He gave an awkward chuckle. "Like I say, there's no knowin' what they'll do or say next."

The woman's rather small eyes suddenly took angry fire against the blackness of her countenance. She made an impatient gesture to throw off Slim's supporting hand. She drew herself fully upright to her five-foot-ten some and announced in that blasting sort of tone of hers:

'My name is Madame Charlotte Amélie Mauricette Elisabeth de Duras. It is a name, sir, that was famous since before the Revolution.''

Bill Cramer was stuck for an immediate answer to that. Finally he mumbled: "Yeh, well, them Injuns only heered the end part, ma'am, I guess ..."

She was still regarding him flashing-eyed, and he realized that some sort of matching courtesy was expected from him by way of introductions.

"I'm William Cramer, ma'am, Deputy U.S. Marshal in charge of this party ridin' out of Fort Smith. This here's Deputy Paul Monkerud. The feller who helped you light down just now is Deputy ... Deputy Huttman. (He couldn't recall what the hell Slim's given name was, and had a feeling he might never have known it in the first place.) And this is Marvin Pollins, also another deputy along with the outfit, ma'am."

Madame de Duras nodded at each of them in turn as they were made known to her, with a kind of tremulous tar-proof dignity. She peered closely at Marv and began talking rapidly in a slight accent.

"This boy has been scalp-taken, yes?" She made a two-handed Gallic gesture at Marv's sore head, shuddering dramatically. "I think all the time I, too, shall *lose my hair*, you say, eh? But they no do that ... Instead –" A tear ran suddenly down the tar. "– instead they do this *unspikable* thing to me ...!"

"Yeh, well, there's plenty enough time to chew

the fat later," Cramer said hastily, taking one of
her slippery arms and beginning to steer her gently
toward the creek. "First off we got to git you clean
of all that sh – muck, ma'am. Oh, it won't take long
and then things mebbe won't seem half so, uh,
black like."

* * *

But that proved to be an over-optimistic statement.

As soon as they got her to the campsite Cramer
thoughtfully ordered Huttman to leave the breakfast fixins to Pollins for that morning, and to stand
by to help him with the more immediate pressing
task. And he curtly told the granite-faced zealot to
go off and see to Kratoch and the animals. For quite
opposite reasons he judged that Pollins and
Monkerud were equally unsuited to assist with
what had to be done.

Slim could appreciate the sense in that approach
to it; but he wasn't looking forward to his own part
one little bit. Madame de Duras now seemed to
have slipped back again into something of her
former apathy as she stood gazing into the fire, and
Slim took advantage of the pause to haul Cramer to
one side for a quiet private talk.

"See here, Billy, there ain't nobody gonna peel
that kind of shit off of her without peelin' *her* the
same time ... You thunk that far ahead?"

Cramer hadn't. Up to this point he had been
thinking only in general terms of a whole lot of
water and a whole lot more of soap, manfully

applied. He swallowed. "Jesus ..."

"Yeh. And when she *is* peeled, what d'you have in mind to cover her back over with? One of they grassy skirts you read about down in them islands? I shouldn't set much store by that idee myself. You any hand at stitchin' grass? I know I ain't, and even if I was there ain't enough growth this year to hide a pigmy woman, leave off one built like her."

Cramer raised a hand to his throbbing forehead. He felt a strong impulse to fog it after the Light Horsemen and tell them bets were off. But he made himself use his head instead.

"How's if we drop a blanket over her, scrub out her rig, dry it in no time in this heat and she puts it right back on?" he suggested none too hopefully.

"Bulljuice ... once that cloth is got off there's no getting it back on. Most likely it'll need to be cut off."

Cramer suddenly snapped his fingers, and began to breathe a shade easier. "The bag – what's in her bag? Bound to be somethin' in there."

The valise had been brought along to the gully, and with a glance of apology at its indifferent owner Cramer knelt and snapped it open. He looked inside, with mounting bewilderment.

On the top was a thick passel of lined paper. Not lined like tablet paper, but sort of in sections of lines, with gaps between. And there were no regular letters along the lines, but all manner of squiggling dots going up and down every whichaway. Cussing beneath his breath, he set the wad of paper aside and rummaged lower down.

As the Choctaw had told them, it was just woman's travelling stuff. Towels, brushes, a few small gewgaws. But then Slim exclaimed over his shoulder: "Lookit that red cloth wi' the poker dots – it's a dress, thank Christ ... Hero, have it out and let's get goin', afore my nerve draws time and drifts the way I kin tell it's apt to do any minute ..."

* * *

The next half hour was one that lingered in the memory of all concerned.

The two of them led Madame de Duras up-creek aways, to a respectable distance from where the other pair were about their given chores. They also took with them a kettle of hot water and a tin bowl, one wagon scrubbing brush, two big chunks of pumice, and six cakes of lye soap; and also the vital red-spotted dress from the valise.

Marvin Pollins, sulkily engaged in cutting up bacon and drysalt meat on the tumbleweed tailgate, almost sliced his thumb off at the noise which suddenly ripped through the trees.

For a wild moment he figured it must be something to do with the hunky, who was now chained up once again to the cedar stump. He grabbed out his handgun and went plunging off in that direction; until a second shattering peal from up-creek fetched him to a halt.

Paul Monkerud came skidding down the bankside, carbine cocked and ready. "What's going on, boy? What was that ruckus, for goshsake?"

A wide grin was now spreading over the younger man's face. He gave an elaborate shrug, seeing a way how he could fun the humorless spook in this situation.

"Aw, it weren't nothin' really, Monk. I mean to say, when you got a case of men on the trail, goin' without women for hours on end ... it ain't a marvel there'd be a sweet caucus when one shows up unexpected, uh? Yes sir ... and there's no saying this one ain't enough to go round two at a time ... I guess you and me together, our crack'll come after breakfast ... I got to admit I admire eatin' first ... how's it with you?"

Monkerud gaped at him so solemnly that he was like to fall down laughing behind his painfully held straight face. Then the zealot gazed furiously past him and up through the long tangle of trees, muttering to himself what Marv took to be Bible scalp music.

The powerful sounds from over yonder had slid down a notch or two by now, with a more passive note to them, and Marv wagged his sore head in the same knowledgeable way.

"Yep, that's one real sweet caucus they got goin', I should say. Almost puts a man's mind off his grub, don't it ..."

He could almost watch the gradual way the spook's blinkered mind was fumbling its way toward the josh. As that slow process was completed, Monkerud went suddenly red in the face.

"Pollins ... you still got a bad lip there, Brother. Don't forget how I fixed it before." He launched him a final eye-bolt of fiery damnation, then wheeled and climbed back up the bank.

Marv chuckled to himself as he carried on with making breakfast, and took a strictly testing spoonful from Slim's jar of lick.

It was a funny thing, but Monkerud didn't bother him half so much now he knew that he was dumb as well as weird and dangerous. The past conversation was still tickling him, and he called over jovially to the prisoner: "How about you, hunky? You feel like havin' a piece of poon along with this bacon?"

Julius Kratoch had a bit more humor in his nature than Paul Monkerud; though not much more. He showed his yellow snaggle teeth in a polite way and asked seriously: "Who is that woman anyway, Deputy? And how did she get in that mess?"

Marv pulled a face as he stirred the beans. "Some high-prancin' stage woman, so the story goes. I don't put much stock in that myself. I think them buck police swoggled us somehow over that part of it. I mean to say, who'd pay a cent to look at her, tar or no tar? It don't make sense, not to me it don't."

He flashed Kratoch a cheerful grin and a wink. "No need for you to ask me questions about her, seein' you'll soon have all the chance in the world to get acquainted. You and she are gonna be riding back to Smith together in the cage."

Kratoch grinned back in the same diplomatic style he had before. But a more experienced set of eyes than the young lawman's might have seen that he was looking rather distracted and thoughtful behind the surface smile.

* * *

Madam Charlotte Amélie Mauricette Elisabeth de Duras came striding fiercely back along the creekbed, with the color of her now visible face heightened to about the same shade as the red dress she had just put on. She held her head high, and she was breathing fast and hard.

Bill Cramer and Slim Huttman followed after her at a safe distance. Slim was saying hollowly: "You know I was on that lousy Goodnight run two-three times? Acrost the desert to the Pecos?"

"What of it?" Cramer rasped shortly. He both looked and felt a distinctly older man that he had half an hour ago. He was certainly in no mood to listen to trailing reminiscences.

"Only I was jes' thinkin' I'd sooner go over it three more times than wash another stage woman free of tar-and-feather. My God, didn' she holler ... You'd of thought we was – you know."

"Yeh, I do know. There's no need to tell me."

"Well, I really figger she did think that, an' all."

"How the hell could she of? How the hell could she take hold of a notion that ridiculous, lookin' the way she was?"

"She couldn't see herself like we could. Anyway, all womenfolks is notional that way," Slim opined grimly. He was hefting a burlap sack which contained the worn-down pumice slabs, the squashed-flat scrubbing brush, and the thin wafers of lye which were all that remained of the cakes of soap after they had literally whaled the tar out of the outraged Frenchwoman.

They halted a moment for Cramor to wipe tar off his barlow knife on a moss-grown rock. "Mebbe I cut her some with this," he grunted moodily. "It was blame hard not to, the way that cloth was like to welded on her skin. Mebbe that was how come she yelled so."

"Nah, you never cut her. It was jes' that she couldn't get it out of her fool head we was after poontang. Lordy, I been hearin' that same kind of unstoppable holler out of good women since I was twelve year old." He paused consideringly. "I allow it all comes from when we's small."

"Small?"

"Yeh. When we ain't yet growed they keep *puttin' us there*, don't they ... Then, after we'se weaned, it don't ever seem quite possible to 'em that we ain't tryin' to git back – even like now through a mess of tar."

*   *   *

Whatever the profound truth of that last theory, it was true enough that Madame de Duras had suspected the motives of the two men who had forcibly washed her.

Nothing so disgraceful had ever happened to her before in the thirty-some years of her existence; not that her life hitherto had been exactly sheltered.

Nearly all of those years had been spent, one way and another, in small touring opera companies, over the length and breadth of the earlier States. Both her parents had been singers, her father having gained a fair reputation in Paris before he came over on tour and decided to stay.

He was of a genuinely illustrious French family, though considered because of his chosen profession as something of a black sheep by it. He hadn't been suited to the New World. Disappointment had gradually overtaken him, followed not long after by drink and death.

Charlotte's mother was an Italian who had been a reliable jobbing singer capable of earning a good living for as long as her voice lasted. Now she was a laundress in Philadelphia.

It was she who had persuaded her daughter to take up the theatrical agency's offer of the engagement in the Choctaw Nation.

"But mama – Indians?" she had said dubiously when the opportunity was first discussed between them.

"I have known some most-a refined Indians," her mother had declared firmly. "Once, in New York, an Indian chief in all his plumes threw flowers on stage after my *Lucia* ... And in any case, child, the performance is for the miners, not the Indians: for my countrymen, living and toiling in the wilderness, thirsting for the culture they once knew ... Come over on Tuesday evening, when I'll be off that dratted late shift, and we'll go through some of my old solo stuff that used-a to knock 'em dead in the good old days before I met your papa."

And indeed the job itself had turned out a big triumph for her. She was well aware that the miners of McAlester would probably have applauded just as much if a strangulated monkey has been there to render their precious *Verdi* and *Donizetti*. But it was one thing to know that, and another to feel the elation of such a whole-hearted reception. A solo career back east had seemed nothing short of inevitable, in those heady moments while she gave them encore after encore.

Charlotte had felt a sense of let-down when it was finally over; and a real urge to give more of herself while she was there. And – fatally – a charming Civilized Tribesman had been among her several admirers clamouring around the stage door; a gentleman who was white in everything but color. He had pleaded with her, positively pleaded, for her to sing to his people at their humble church meeting, before she returned to the east.

Recalling her mama's good impressions of the long-ago native *Lucia*-lover, she had graciously agreed to that request for what was plainly to be a charity performance. Normally neither she nor her parent much cared for them; but it had seemed only right to Charlotte that she should give her art freely to the people whose land this was.

Her success at the Indian meeting had exceeded even that of her official booking. She had given the packed little place a mixed repertoire, uncertain as to their particular taste; but each offering was received with near-hysterical adulation by the men present. They had been mostly men in the meeting hall. Charlotte had begun to see what her mother had meant about the Indians' capacity for cultural improvement.

... But then she made the acquaintance of their wild and malevolent womenfolk. And, later, that of their unsympathetic and almost hostile policemen. The trail had then led her remorselessly to this terrible washing at the hands of the two (she would swear) lecherous-minded federal marshals ...

She flung herself down haughtily by the primitive cooking-fire; gazing at first blindly, but then with a fresh tremor of alarm, at the crouched figure of Julius Kratoch who was once again chained to the cedar trunk nearby.

NINE

Her alarm soon changed to indignation. Marvin Pollins was approaching the fire at that moment with a batch of bread for frying and she snapped at him:

"You, sir! Kindly inform me the reason why that poor man is in chains ..."

Marv stooped down to arrange the pan bread in the already spitting skillet. Then he straightened and kicked the fire inward a little and faced his questioner with frank and dispassionate interest.

It seemed to him that Bill and Slim had done a pretty fair job on her, given the tough circumstances. At least you could see her face now, even if it had turned out to be homely and not all that worth the scraping. He didn't reckon they'd quite got there with her hairdo: though you could tell now it was more sorrel than black it was still hanging down in dulled coils of tar, and still had the odd chicken feather scattered in it like a weird decoration. And peeling the tar off the rest of her hadn't made her look thinner any. With those feathers still on her, and the fatness, and the settled fractious look that a man could see clearly now, she looked to him for all the world like a harpy Comanche squaw.

Marv pulled his roving thoughts back in line. "You mean the hunky, ma'am?"

"I do not know this word ... I mean *him*."

"Sure. That's Kratoch," Marv told her uneasily. "He's locked to that stump on account of he's apt to hie off if he weren't so, ma'am."

Just then Julius Kratoch gave one of his deep and rattling lung-coughs, and Madame de Duras's face grew more fractious still. "But he is *ill* ... I know the texture of that sound. I am sensitive to all sound. He has the consumption, yes?"

Marv pulled a wry face as he knelt to turn the bread and to nudge the adjoining pan of bacon.

"It's a job to know at times if he's sick or he ain't. He'll go and spit blood ever' so often. But he's got enough puff in him when he feels like it to shin up a six foot judge and bust down the timber. We wouldn't of had the bother of follerin' him here if he couldn't do things like that. And was you to hand him a scattergun and watch him run behint that, you wouldn't think he was ailing, I tell you. That's if he hadn't filled your Goddam – uh, beggin' your pardon – that's if he hadn't filled your skull with lead so's you couldn't figger one way or the other about this here hunky's state of health."

Madame de Duras studied Kratoch with a touch more of reserve and less of compassion. Kratoch coughed again and gave her a faint grin with his discolored teeth.

"What is this word you keep calling him: this *hunky*, eh?"

Marv stared; then got her. "Well, like bohunk, ma'am."

Her brow stayed furrowed, then suddenly cleared. "Ah! He is Bohemian, yes?" She gave Kratoch a more thorough inspection. "Yes, I can see now that he is."

She increased her voice so that it carried effortlessly over to the prisoner. "Mister Kratoch, I have a good friend who is also Bohemian like you – a fine violinist who plays *obbligato* for me sometimes. His name is Capek, Victor Capek. Maybe you know him?"

The polite grin was suddenly gone from Kratoch's sharp-boned face. He glowered at her, rattling his shackles in an angered way.

"I'm Czech, ma'am. Not Bohemian. Czech," he repeated fussily. 'And I don't know your pal."

Marvin Pollins added more wood to the fire, shuttling a bewildered glance between the pair of them as he did so. He could barely catch their drift, but just enough to understand that Madame de Duras was still woefully ignorant about the stripe of jigger they had on the chain-up tree. He felt she ought to be straightened out about him if they were due to travel together, her not being a criminal at all and plainly not knowing one when she saw him. He made another earnest try at opening her eyes.

"Kratoch here's a whiskey runner, ma'am. He don' play violins or nothin' like that. He's a good hand with a corn still and that's about it. He's poisoned half the Nations in his time. When the old judge gits him back again he'll give him a ten year pull if it's a day."

What this dumb stage woman finally made of that Marvin hadn't time to tell, for Bill and Slim were returning by now from up-creek and he had to quit jawing and snap to it with the breakfasts. But he had a feeling that she still wasn't looking on the hunky in the sharp-minded way it would pay her to.

She seemed to want to act sort of kindly toward him ... Lord alone knew why. But most likely a spell of his company in the tumbleweed would soon take care of that, he reasoned more optimistically as he hurried back to the tailgate.

* * *

Cramer hadn't been looking forward to telling Madame de Duras that he planned for her to travel in the prison wagon. From what he'd now learned of her nature he didn't think she would take it too well.

But there was no help for it. Since Monkerud's horse had been shot from under him and he was using the spare saddle animal, Charlotte de Duras either had to ride with Kratoch or else pack double with one or other of the rest of them. The way she was feeling now toward Slim and himself, he couldn't see her choosing either of them for close company. If he was to put her up behind Monkerud, the zealot would be fit to be tied; and if he was to put her behind Marv Pollins that lippy lad would no doubt offend her female sensitivity some other way than it had been already. So he reckoned the tumbleweed it had to be, whether she was wishful of it or not.

He put it to her when they were breaking camp.

"I know it ain't befittin' for you to ride with the hunky, ma'am, but the way we're fixed for horses it's about the best I can do."

She regarded him with the dark suspicion she had shown to him ever since she was washed. "Am I to be in chains also?" she enquired acidly.

"Shucks, no. Kratoch won't be in them either once he's in the rig. But I will need to lock you in with him. But don't fret over that, were he to try anything we'd soon keep him in line, ma'am."

To his astonishment she then agreed to it quite meekly.

"... anyway I quite like Mister Kratoch. He is a man of ancient culture – I can feel it," she said firmly as she strode off with her plunder bag toward the wagon.

Slim came up behind him with an armful of pans and metal spiders. "What's that she come out with then?" the driver murmured.

Cramer let out a low whistle. "Just lettin' me know that our hunky's a man of culture. I guess what she meant to say is he stacks up pretty good with her next to us two ravishers. Women," he added harshly, "you can't win with them."

Slim Huttman kept to a tactful silence. He knew that the woman now on his partner's mind was Helen Cramer and not Charlotte de Duras. To turn him off that sore subject he said: "Madame Thing ain't one of Kratoch's tribe though, is she?"

"Shouldn't think she is. That's a French name, when they have a *de* before the end of it. But she's knocked around with hunkies before, accordin' to what Marv heard 'em say together backalong. Maybe that means they'll stay civil to each other in the cage till we can get 'em back. Anyway, the hell with them both, let's be rolling."

The mules hit their collars and they dragged out of the gully on the start of the haul back to Arkansas.

Pollins and Monkerud rode on the south side of the rig, Cramer on the side which faced to the not-far-distant but invisible line of the Canadian, which divided the northern Choctaw Nation from the Creek country. As usual, it became very hot by ten o'clock in the morning. Dust devils began to spin across the old military road which they were using now for the return journey.

Madame de Duras was seated on one of the wagon's long sideboards. She had fished a blue sunbonnet out of her valise, and it was pulled down casually over her mass of tangled and still sticky hair. It made a vivid contrast with the red dress, but she seemed to be the sort of woman who was unaware of details like that. She was perspiring like the rest of them, now and then fanning her face with one of her large and be-ringed hands.

Julius Kratoch ignored her. He lay sprawled out on his mattress in the centre of the box, coughing occasionally and hawking at the tailgate. Most of

the time he was gazing in a morose way back where
they had come from, breathing in and out all the
while in his rapid and shallow fashion.

Charlotte de Duras had been gazing pensively at
the more southerly scenery through the mesh of the
cage, for some miles past. But now she broke the
long silence between them. "That cough, my friend
... it will kill you, you know that?"

Kratoch jerked his bony head round, looking over
at her with eyes that were swimming with fever
again, and hot with something other than just the
temperature within and outside him.

"You aimin' to tell me something, ma'am? You
think I ain't got the sense to know I'm in a way to
cashin' in?" He sent another jet of spittle out
through the end of the rig.

Madame de Duras gave a twitch of disgust. She
was about to speak strongly to Kratoch when the
tumbleweed lurched up one side on an outcrop,
causing him to lose his air of dour resignation and
yell out in protest.

"Hey – you bum on the seat! Can't you handle
this thing any better than this? Godamighty!"

"– and yet, your lungs are still not as sick as they
might be," Charlotte continued calmly, as if there
had been no vulgar interuption to their talk. "Or
you would not be able to use that much volume to
shout with."

Kratoch flashed her a resentful jeering glare.
"You some sorta woman medicine doc when you
ain't tar-and-feathered? You got a passel of Sear
Roebuck cures there in your bag?"

"No I haven't. I'm a singer," she replied evenly.

He gave a bitter bray of amusement, ending in another bout of racking coughs. "... Then you kin butt out of my affairs!" he said snarlingly when it was over. "I don't need singin' to right now. Later, mebbe."

He pulled a grim, hopeless face, not bothering to look at her any more while they spoke. Once again his eyes were fixed dully on the shimmering western prairie they were leaving behind.

"That's just where you're wrong, Mister Kratoch. I know exactly what you should do with those lungs – *use them*! I know what I am talking about. People in my profession hardly ever develop consumption. That is a medically accepted fact."

Julius Kratoch fetched his eyes back inside the rig with a long final sigh of defeat. He met Charlotte's remorseless good will toward him with a kind of weary patience.

"Look, lady, I dassay you means well. But I been usin' these bad lungs all my life so far, believe it or not. And where the old judge is certain-sure gonna send me, which is Ohio again, I know from before that it ain't dry enough to suit me that far east. I only kept in front of the posse they sent after me lately due to the rare heat we been gettin' this summer. And I only headed these here half-ass marshals as far as I did for the same reason. But my string's plumb run out now, and there's no use in –"

His flow of guttural and mournful talk was all of a sudden shut right off. Once again he was looking through the closed tailgate. Looking there very

intently now. But Charlotte de Duras was far too
taken up with her certainty that she could cure him
to notice his abrupt change of manner.

"Nonsense!" she was saying robustly. "It is
purely a matter of *correct breathing*. Now, Mister
Kratoch – watch me breathe ..."

She sat up straighter on the sideboard, and for no
apparent reason her sizable belly began to balloon
outward to a still greater rotundity. Then she let
the air out of her with a rush.

"You see ...? But when *you* breathe, it is always
up *here* ..." She thumped her well-covered stern-
um. "That is no good. Disease takes a hold in the
stagnant space underneath, you follow? Now, I
want you to ..."

She became crossly aware that this difficult pupil
wasn't paying her proper attention. And then, to
her amazement, several things seemed to happen
all at once, none of them connected with her
theories for improving Kratoch's health.

First, and to her shock and alarm, the sickly
prisoner came up off his mattress with the speed of
a striking copperhead and crashed bodily into her
on the sideboard.

His small and reduced frame could have weighed
only a fraction of her own bulk, but the sheer speed
and force of it was enough to shove her the few
inches off the seatboard so that she floundered
down into the box.

Julius Kratoch then somehow worked his skeletal
form almost underneath her with a wriggling,
burrowing intensity, while all the while grabbing

hold of her with astonishing strength. And at the same time he was bawling out close to her left ear:

— *"Ladi*! *Karel*! Shoot up the rig, boys! I'm covered! Drill the driver and bust the cage lock, then I'm loose, I ain't shackled! Shoot where you like – I'm covered!"

By the time Charlotte had pulled her stunned mind back to a sense of what was happening, strange men and horses were careening everywhere around the tumbleweed, and a volley of shots was humming close by – very close by! It occurred to her that these attackers were taking the treacherous, craven Czech at his word and enfilading the wagon space with bullets while he cowered beneath her in safety!

None of the bullets appeared to strike her, however. The pattern of shooting seemed to be altering now, becoming more ragged and interspersed with return fire from the lawmen. She didn't dare to look up but had a feeling that the attack was being beaten off. Her initial fright began to subside. She was still shaking and trembling; but now with a kind of deep betrayed rage.

TEN

It was Paul Monkerud who saved the day when the rest of them were caught napping.

The zealot had never been happy about the 'coincidence' of Kratoch making a stand so near to the Cross Timbers. Even after that wild and lawless region was left well behind them he had continued to brood about it as he rode drag after the tumbleweed on its south flank.

Not that it was his only concern just now; he was still by no means reconciled to the flagrant affront to the Almighty that Cramer had so recklessly given by letting the stage woman ride with Kratoch in this brazen fashion.

Ever since they'd commenced their return journey Monkerud had been riding in constant dread of seeing a great fiery lance come striking down at the wagon – quite conceivably from the hand of a visible avenging angel, if the affront was considered serious enough. He gave a sombre nod as he rode along; recollecting a time back in Kansas when he had witnessed an avenging angel doing just that once before, after he'd known it was on the cards.

That piece of retribution had been to do with only a minor case of a hayrick made on a Sunday. The angel had simply fired the rick with its lance and been willing to let it go at that. But it was plumb obvious they could be in for a mighty bigger retribution for something as bad as this ...

But even while that closed side of his mind was thus occupied, the ordinary workaday lawman side of it was still ferreting on about that sharp-minded hunky, and the way he *could* have been heading for the Cross Timbers before his horse foundered. And it was that normal side of Paul Monkerud which had taken a warning jolt when the tumbleweed itself was jolted on the rock outcrop.

He noticed then that the outcrop was on the end of a low limestone ridge which curved off south-west of the wagon road, forming a long straggled arc through the grass. It wouldn't give any bushwhackers much cover ... but some. Enough. And if any hardcases should be following after them from the Cross Timbers, the shape of the ridge would be right handy for them to do that unseen.

But by the time he had thought of the possible danger the wagon had passed by the obvious ambush point. So – nothing to worry about. Nothing at all. To his surprise, however, he still found himself sliding his rifle out of the saddleboot.

Five seconds later and he was firing it like a sewing machine at the several men who'd spilled belatedly out of the rocks, and who were now kneeling and firing directly into the wagon bed.

... Only the Almighty Himself knew why the bushwhackers had passed up the chance to hit them sooner ... But this was one of those rare moments in his life when Monkerud didn't wait to ponder on the designs of the Almighty. Instead, he wrenched his animal around and set it straight for the raiders at a dead run, shooting and levering as he came at them.

Through the racket of explosions he heard Pollins's claybank pounding close behind him, then saw that big rawboned plug from the edge of his eye as it streaked across to defend the rig from the better defence-point of the mules' end. Marv's carbine spat red. Cramer was starting up too now from the north of the rig.

But it was his own faster reaction that was actually knocking men over, putting men down ... Most of the bunch seemed insanely unaware that he was doing it to them, continuing to rake the wagon with fire, almost with their backs to him ... Two of them, though, suddenly jerked their heads around and he caught an impression of their panicking faces: pale, sharp-boned, dark-eyed ... Still jacking and firing like an automaton, he thought hazily: *bohunks like Kratoch*. But he was too keyed up to be able to make the connection.

One of those who had so lately looked away from their target now swivelled what could have been a Remington at him as he tried to ride the man down. The bang of it deafened him on that side, the slug plucking at his shirt-sleeve. The man then skittered aside as the horse plunged in on him, but

Monkerud hauled its head around to the left and the offside haunch slammed into the bushwhacker and his heavy rifle tossed up in the air as he went down. Monkerud fired at him, too hastily, missed, and was then forced to fire at another one of them by the time he'd jacked up another shell.

He caught that one neatly in the throat, and the one he had missed struggled half-upright, grabbing for his revolver, and then went down finally as a bullet from Huttman up on the wagon seat took him in the head.

Then Cramer and Pollins came storming around both sides of the rig and the three of them were close-shooting with the remainder of the would-be rescuers of Julius Kratoch.

… They were gutsy, those few surviving pals of the whiskey runner. They were now caught clear in the open between a deadly triangle of guns. Monkerud kept hearing Bill Cramer bawling at them to quit, but it was quite clear to him, at least, from the way they held themselves, that quitting wasn't in their scheme of things.

Shooting still was, though … Pollins's claybank was pin-wheeling one second and flat down the next, with its round-faced rider dropping off nimbly behind it and poking the snout of his saddlegun promptly over its heaving ribs, using it as a breastwork.

Then there was only one hunky-lover left on his feet. The man took in that fact as Cramer yelled again for him to give up. Then he half-shrugged and gave a lop-sided berserker's grin, and snapped off a last suicide round at the lawdog who'd given him that contemptible choice.

The three of them blasted him so near in, and so close together, that he seemed to lift straight off the ground as if the three bullets were pinning him there. Then he came finally out of his rifleman's crouch and sort of rolled out on the sod.

Cramer sat there in his hull for another long second behind the smoking carbine; then slammed it back in the boot and shakily got down. He walked over to the last of the dead heroes and kicked his head into a more identifiable position. He stood over him a moment, swaying, then said in a curious cracked voice: "Paul ... wouldn' you say this bird was Laddy Huss?"

Monkerud usually got his control back quite fast at times like this. He got down and joined the head deputy as Marv Pollins began to wobble upright from behind the claybank. A minute later all three of them looked down upon the last raider to die.

Monkerud said composedly: "Yeh, that's Huss all right. Why d'you reckon one like him was buyin' in for a no-account like Kratoch?"

Cramer made no immediate answer to that. He had now moved off to inspect another of the bunch. Pollins said in a whisper: "Shit, Monk, how many *was* there of 'em, come to that?" He gazed blindly about him.

"Seven," Monkerud told him, after solemnly counting. "Seven ... and you know somethin'? They've all got a samey look to 'em, ain't they ..." He bared his teeth in a harsh grin of dawning comprehension. "*Hey, Cramer!* Did you ever hear tell that Laddy Huss was some brand of bohunk hisself?"

Cramer was just straightening up from examining the fourth of them by this time. All four fetched dead ... And he had a strong instinct from the stillness of the other three that they were just the same.

He shook his head in dumbfoundment. Sure, there'd been a mess of lead in the air, but it didn't really account for it. He had been in several fights in the Territory before now of much the same fierceness as this one. But such a hundred-per-cent lethal outcome was a new experience for him; especially as their own side was weirdly unhurt.

He peered through the reeking pall of gunsmoke, which had hardly shifted yet in the windless heat. He couldn't get over it. These men had been hit in all manner of places – but every one of them mortal. His glazed eyes blinked to a focus. Why, even Marv's horse there looked to be stone dead too. Today, he gathered, was a day when it didn't matter what species you belonged to – you only had to be hit to be dead ...

He had only half-heard Monkerud's question, and had to shake his head and think about it before replying. Then he said tonelessly: "No, I never did hear that. But I can think of someone who might be able to tell us."

The three of them marched grimly up to the bullet-scarred tailgate and looked inside the cage.

They saw Julius Kratoch lying in a heap in a front corner, and Madame de Duras standing in the middle of the box with her brawny arms held akimbo and her heavy face quivering with emotion.

Slim had stayed up on the seat all this while. His old Winchester was still slightly fuming – and now he held it tilted down at Charlotte de Duras.

He said dryly: "That was some battle. Quite a one been goin' on here in the meantime, too. Madam here took a notion to belt the hunky a good one after he aimed to use her hide to winter under. Come ta that, she belted him three times. Then I figgered she orta be ree-strained." He waggled the long barrel reproachfully at the pent-up Frenchwoman.

Cramer turned aside to Marv Pollins. "Go look for their horses up the ridge." Then he unlocked the gate and jumped up inside.

He went over to the crumpled, weeping hunky in the corner and took hold of his pointed chin with his fingers and clawed him up to a sitting position with the one hand.

Kratoch left off blubbering in a hurry and let out a reedy cry of pain. He shrank back from the deputy's granite face, fearful of torture. Behind the two of them Charlotte de Duras uttered some violent exclamation, but Slim Huttman drawled from above: "Easy, ma'am ... jes' let nature tek its course."

"Now you better tell it to me, shitbag," Cramer said softly. "Are you some kin to Laddy Huss?"

Kratoch tried to glare back at him but couldn't quite make it.

"Yeh ... cousins," he ground out bitterly.

"Then how come he ain't got that kind of moniker?"

"Huss *is* a Czech name, Marshal," Kratoch wheezed up at him. "Not all of us has what you think of as dumb hunky names like mine. Huss is a regular Czech name, take my word."

Cramer considered that answer suspiciously. He grunted: "*Your word* ... Laddy sure ain't a foreign name. I've known plenty of Americans called Laddy."

"It is too! It don't end with a Y the way you people hear it. It's L-A-D-I. Standin' for Ladislas."

Bill Cramer eased off a bit from squeezing his chin. But he still had him in a fairly persuasive pinch. "I see ... Have you got any more famous outlaw cousins? Or *did you have*, I should say?" He gave a jerky wave at the bodies littering the prairie. " 'Cause they-all have a strong look of your selfsame buggerin' tribe. *Well*?" He tweaked him more sharply again.

"*Aah*! No, Marshal ... Leastways, Huss is – was – the only one who's my ackshal kinfolks. But there's one more out there I know of. That's Karel Skoda. Him nearest the rig. He used to live in the Kiamichis near my place, then he got in some trouble and went on the scout. I guess Ladislas pulled him in to lend a hand."

"Damn nice of him. How did you know there'd be a bunch waitin' to side you in the Cross Timbers?"

"Ladislas sent me word in jail, by a Choctaw witness for another case. The message said if I could manage to bust loose and get that far, he'd take care of any federal bast – any federals comin' after me."

"So your horse, meanin' the horse you grabbed, foundered a shade too soon, uh?" Cramer grinned at him without sympathy. "And so you had to do your best on your own till they heard on the Injun telegraph and came to locate you. Not that it weren't a salty enough best at that," he added grudgingly.

He chewed it over, then looked back at him with a renewal of suspicion. "Laddy Huss didn't make a habit of runnin' with low-grade badmen who couldn't even rig an ambush right. Why did he this time?"

Kratoch showed a brief flare of spirit. "They was high-grade enough to die tryin', Marshal!" He sagged back to the dulled bitterness again and went on more quietly and wearily: "It could of been this way, Mister Cramer. Like maybe Ladislas Huss couldn't talk his regular outfit into riskin' their necks just for a Czech bootlegger. That could answer you why those men out there who's died for me ain't what you call high-grade badmen. Could be they were just a bunch of hard-luck Czechs like me who Ladi hazed into doin' it out of loyalty mostly, I shouldn't wonder." His tears were running again as he looked back on it in that moving fashion.

"Gwan ... Since when did you scum know the meanin' of loyalty?" Cramer scoffed. But privately he was thinking that could be about the truth of it; or the half-truth, if Huss had paid out a few bucks for it as well. To his experienced eye those bodies lying on the grass had the look of bodies who'd been paid at least something to risk getting that way.

He let go of Kratoch and swung up and around to face Charlotte de Duras. She was now half-sitting awkwardly on the short round metal stanchion in the centre of the wagon box, to which the big chain was normally fastened when the cage was fully loaded with dangerous shackled criminals. As he took a step toward her he could see Marv coming back along the ridge, with seven good-looking saddle animals trotting ahead of him.

Cramer brightened, for that welcome sight made it easier to say what he had in mind to the madame here.

"You OK, ma'am?" He saw that her slab cheeks were still quivering like twin jellies.

She gave a mute nod. Then: "But I should not have struck Mister Kratoch in anger, as I did. I should have remembered that he is sick," she murmured low-voiced. She shook her untidy blue-bonneted head remorsefully.

"Yeh, well, that's a thing it pays a body to forget with Kratoch. Trouble is, when he ain't ailing he's inclined to be dynamite. I shouldn't bother too much over it, ma'am. Anyway, there's no need now for you to travel with him for the rest of the trip. At least them hellions had some decent horses. You can take one of 'em and use it to go on to Smith."

She looked at him in a blank and uninterested way. "If it's the same to you, Mister Cramer, I'll stay where I am." She gave an odd little smile, then gazed past him to stare fixedly at the still weeping Czech. "I think perhaps that is my duty after I struck him when, after all, he was only afraid: only running to me for protection because he was afraid."

Cramer gaped at her. It seemed to him that was the damndest way of describing Kratoch's try at using her carcass to soak up his pals' bullets. But he hadn't the time just now to dwell on female fractiousness. He said curtly: "Fine. If you change your mind, let me know and we'll rig out one of this outlaw cavvy for you like I said."

* * *

Only, as he might have guessed, that wasn't fine at all; not by Paul Monkerud it wasn't.

The zealot was standing like a stiff tall crane amongst the dead bushwhackers when Cramer went up to him, and his face was not all that healthier in color than theirs.

"Bill – you've got to get that woman out of the rig – *immediate!*" Monkerud told him with hissing fervour.

Cramer sighed. "I just tried to, but she won't hear of it. She'd sooner ride on with Kratoch than take an outlaw nag."

He was startled when Monkerud suddenly laid hold of his arm in a vise-like grip. "But don't you see ... don't *even you* finally see what this means?" He gestured at the seven corpses with a kind of fearful awe.

"I see we were plumb lucky to nail them," Cramer murmured uneasily. "That was down to you mostly, Paul. I got to admit you was some awaker than the rest of us when they hit."

The zealot brushed that compliment impatiently aside. He began to explain himself as if to a slow-witted child.

"Jes' think about it: all those seven, struck dead with mostly the one shot each and no more ... don't you see now? We had *her in the cage wi' him*! It's a Sign, Brother! A merciful Sign that we been granted jes' one more chance not to flout the Almighty! I beg of you, Brother – git her out of there while there's still time!"

Bill Cramer felt his remaining small stock of patience running out as surely as if he were a human sand-glass. He said tightly: "We been into all that before. The woman ain't done nothin' wrong and can travel how she likes. Aw, I know, I know ... on my head be it. Now, was there something else you wanted to say before we roll again?"

Monkerud scorched him with his crazy hot coals for a long tense moment. Cramer didn't care worth a damn right then whether he would have to throw down on him or not. He'd had a bait of Paul Monkerud this trip. Maybe the zealot sensed that barely-contained wildness in him. At any rate he finally seemed to slack off.

But another prickly side of his complex nature now came to the fore – the man of thrift.

"Yeh, there was somethin' else. We're taking Laddy Huss back for scalp money," he stated firmly, without allowing any question of it.

Cramer pursed his lips but was really glad of this chance to go along with him. "I guess so. The Colonel said we shouldn't take up any live prisoners on the swing. But Huss ain't alive and I reckon we're due for what's on him after survivin' a bee like that. What was on him anyway at last count?"

"Fifteen hundred," Monkerud told him in businesslike tones. "It went up after Parker pressured the railroad company when Huss pulled that express car job back in the winter."

"Right. We'll tie him over one of the broncs they came on and he goes back with us."

"Him and the rest, Bill. They may be nobodys but there's enough to amount up worthwhile."

Cramer stared wonderingly at the grasping man of God.

"I've got a feelin' you ain't thought it through," he told him heavily. "Look, if we go back to Smith ahead of seven cadavers on seven nags follering after, we ain't gonna look like field deputies comin' in from a tumbleweed run – we're gonna look like an oldtime Army patrol crawlin' back from Comancheria!"

Monkerud's face stiffened into rock-stubborn, deadly lines. His hand moved a quarter-inch toward his gun-rig. "I want my portion on them all," he said flatly.

Cramer took a hitch on his temper and made himself think about it rationally. Rationally, there was one point much against them leaving the deceased hunkies here on the Prairie Plains. Namely that they couldn't pile rocks on them this

far off the mountains, and the ground would be
almost impossible to dig in after all the heat. By the
time they did get them planted they would have
burned a hell of a lot of daylight and energy doing
it. He also reminded himself that he owed
Monkerud for still being alive, however aggravating
he was.

"OK," he said thinly. "They all go back. But
don't hook me any more this trip, Paul, for I'm
getting tired of it."

ELEVEN

They travelled more slowly with the burdened six-string plodding after the tailgate. One of the bushwhackers' animals was having to pack two corpses to leave a replacement mount available for Pollins.

Cramer had aimed earlier for a nooning back on the Brushy, but the sun was middle down before they raised the banks of that drouthy trickle once again and slogged wearily along its course to their former campsite.

They were all done in after the fighting and then the extended journey through the heat. Slim Huttman wobbled about on rubber legs tending to the mules, while the other lawmen sprawled out full-length in the scanty shade from the withered leaves overhead.

Julius Kratoch had turned a sicklier shade than usual about the face and lips, and his breath was now rasping loud enough to carry over to the group of exhausted men from the piece off where they had parked the rig. Charlotte de Duras had objected in strong terms to them chaining him up outside. She was still in the cage section with him now, patiently dribbling water between Kratoch's crooked teeth and getting him to try her breath exercises.

They heard him raising strong objections to that line of treatment at one point.

"Leave off pawin' my belly! There ain't nothin' amiss with me down there, you damnfool woman! Look, you wanta make yourself useful you kin go and strike them Goddam marshals for a quirly. That's what I crave for right now, not your crazy ideas ..."

"No, Julius, that I cannot permit. Smoking is hard enough on good lungs. For yours, it is out of the question from now on. Now, shall we try once more? Take another slow, deep breath down to get some air where it will do the most good. Which means – *here*."

"Bugger off ...!"

However, a moment later they heard him making a different sort of rattle that sounded as if he were obeying instructions.

Marv's drawn young face cracked into a faint grin. "That stage woman, she's got the hunky dancin' to her toon like a li'll feist dog. Whyinhell's she bothering to? She too dumb to know her blubber'd be cookin' right now on the prairie if he'd had any say in it?"

Bill Cramer shifted his chewing over. It seemed to take a huge effort of tongue and jaws. "She feels badly for slappin' him around back at the fight, that's why she's tendin' him now."

Slim had come nearby to clear their old ash out of the fire-pit when he was saying that. He looked over and drawled: "You reckon?"

Cramer blinked back at the driver-cook and gave a mighty yawn.

"Sure. She good as said so. Anyhow, you should know, you was watchin' him and her back then more than us busy boys had the time to."

Slim wavered upright again. "Seed her belt him, that's true," he murmured thoughtfully. "Somehow put me a-mind of how my old ma used to belt pappy now an' then." He gave an engimatic nod and started to set the kindling; doing so in his former offhand and conscripted fashion. He had lost his enthusiasm for being a late-discovered wonder cook; this latest stop had reminded him what he'd known all along: that cooks were just idiots who had to stay working while sensible men rested.

Cramer tried to follow the eyebrow trail of meaning in what Slim had said then, but couldn't. He gave up on it and mumbled heavily: "Sweet Jesus, the thought of a fire now is just too much ... I feel one lick of extry flame will finish me after burnin' out all day long. Look, can't you knock out some cold grub for us? Then you could build just a small coffee fire as night comes on."

"Sure I could, 'cepting that madame says that *Julius* – yeh, *Julius* – needs a proper hot meal after the hard time he's done had. And never mind if this is the hottest day of this whole consarn summer. So that's what *Julius* is gonna have. And if he's gettin' it you better believe that you ranahans get the same." He limped off to the wagon for his gear, still muttering.

Marv Pollins rolled over off his back and said: "That Kratoch ... My Gawd he knows how to survive, don' he." He gave a high over-strained laugh. "First he stands on the old judge, then he leaves a posse to crap theirselves, then he tries blastin' us fellers to bits, then his cousins come and try the same thing ... and what happens to *him*? He winds up with madame there showin' him ways to keep his lungs goin' strong and happy to nurse him like a dogy. I dunno. Monk, you's the man with religion – kin you explain how come this asswipe in the cage has that kinda hand dealt out to him every game he sets in?"

But for once the zealot was unable to answer either the point of theology or Marvin's forgetful bad language when in his presence. For, as Pollins now observed with a wry satisfaction, both the older men beside him were in dreamland. It was a short-lived triumph, since a few seconds later he joined them there.

*   *   *

The three of them turned in early that night; and by next morning they were still not fully awake by the usual time that Cramer had the outfit up and about. Then, however, they shed their blankets as fast as men could, and with their pistols coming out before they were even upright.

"*Holy shit wassat?*" Pollins gasped out, aiming his handgun at everything inside his circle of vision. Monkerud, reacting faster to the source of the weird sound, plunged up the bankside toward the rig.

"Yep: it's gotta be another go at bustin' Kratoch loose ... c'mon, *move!*" Cramer snapped at Pollins as he floundered after the zealot.

Another of the extraordinary series of noises which had awoken them ripped from the wagon as they crashed through the brush. And then another ...

Cramer saw Monkerud ahead of him brake to a sudden uncertain halt. And then he himself belatedly understood that this was no further assault on the tumbleweed as he'd figured.

Those noises were coming from the thick gullet of Charlotte de Duras. She was sitting on the lowered tailgate, in the act of tipping a panful of hot beans on to a tin plate. A crispy piece of bacon was already on it. And Kratoch was down on the ground, *unchained*, leaning back against the nigh-side front wheel.

Cramer shoved Monkerud aside and clink-clumped over to her.

"What's all this ruckus about?" he enquired tersely. "And how come the prisoner's runnin' around loose from the cage?"

Madame de Duras looked up with a bright, merry sort of smile.

"Good morning, Marshal. I trust you feel restored after your long rest, you and the other pair who were so wonderfully brave yesterday."

Bill Cramer was no longer the sort of man who could be syruped by the female sex. Helen Cramer had taken any such weakness away from him at the time when she'd pulled out. "Who gave you permission to unlock the hunky? I thought I made it clear last night that if you chose to be locked in with him then there you stayed till I let you out."

"Mr Huttman gave permission," she returned placidly, setting eating tools on the plate and taking it over to Kratoch who received it with a baleful glare and no word of thanks. She came back from him and went on: "You see, it was necessary that Julius had his nourishment before you and the other poor men this morning, since you were all naturally so tired. So Mr Huttman kindly fetched the key from by your bedroll and let us out."

"Did he now. I'll talk to him presently about that." He looked at her with rising exasperation. "Look, Kratoch ain't to be trusted, Madame Duras, ain't you got that plain enough fact through your skull yet?"

"I agree, Marshal," she said in a serious way that was somehow not at all reassuring. "There are certain aspects of Julius's character which – at present, anyway – are clearly far from satisfactory and even disturbing. That is why Mr Huttman is sitting over yonder there, with his rifle at the ready."

She waved a plump arm up at the edge of the nearby creek bank, to a place where Slim's Levi'd legs were comfortably dangling over. His long-snouted old '63 gave off a blue wink in the bright morning sunlight beyond the gully. He nodded down sardonically at the confused trio of late risers. "Afternoon, boys."

"Oh ... that's OK then," Cramer said back to her lamely. Partly to change the subject he glanced sidewise and mumbled: "Kratoch seems a mite more chipper today if I don't miss my guess." He looked back at her with reluctant approval. "Your tendin' him's done some good."

"Yes, he is distinctly better, through my application of a little correct breathing." Her large face suddenly grinned. "You would not have heard me doing my scales otherwise."

"Your what, ma'am?"

"Scales. Voice practice. I do them every morning of my life for a full hour without fail, unless there is some real crisis to prevent it like my encounter with those primitive Indian women. Of course, if Julius had still been sinking, that would have been another such crisis and my scales would once again have had to 'remain unsung' to so speak. Ha-ha!"

"You mean to say you been makin' that – doin' that scales for an *hour* and we never heered you till the finish?" Cramer grunted in frank disbelief.

She gave another short bellow of laughter. "Oh no, I've only just started! Tell me, are you and your companions at all musical?"

"Our line a work there's not much call to be," he told her shortly.

"What a pity. Julius is extremely musical, I fancy. But then, all his people are, their culture is such an ancient one. I'd imagine he is also a good businessman, wouldn't you say, Marshal?"

He looked again over at Kratoch, who sent him a feeble trapped-looking snarl in return. It slowly came to him then that this hunky was still in shackles all right ... It was just that you couldn't see them quite as well as before.

"Well, ma'am, far as I know he never had much trouble fixin' a high price for his green whiskey. I guess you could say he was businesslike in that way."

Madame de Duras seemed encouraged by that qualified answer.

"I thought so! What a shame he has to go to jail ... Right now I stand sorely in need of a first-rate, cultured business manager, to safeguard me from making stupid errors of judgement such as the one which has marred the success of my recent engagement."

"Right now, ma'am," he told her patiently, "you and the rest of us needs to get to Fort Smith. You can do the rest of your sing-song along the way. As for Kratoch he's got a, uh, urgent business appointment with Judge Parker."

* * *

A little later their long procession was stretched out back on the old Army road.

Cramer wanted to make the line of the hills by the time the heat grew unbearable again. That happened a little earlier each day now. It soon stopped the madame from her caterwauling, as he'd reckoned it would.

By ten a.m. the sketchy zigzag of the Sansbois first showed on the horizon. And, also by that time, the bodies of the hunky's pals were starting to make their presence felt as a following breeze picked up; a breeze which carried the stench but was entirely baked out of cooling properties.

Cramer mopped his face as the mountains kept coming and going through the haze. "Can't you whup them up a bit more?" he called to the driver.

"They's whupped out same as we all are, Billy."

Slim's laconic reply was the plain truth of it. Getting Kratoch back in front of Isaac Parker had proved a tough and testing assignment for man and beast alike.

Still, Cramer told himself, as he eased on to his other equally numb buttock in the molten vise of his saddle, it was all but over now. Only a few more miles of this and he and the rest of the outfit would be blowing down a raft of celebration beers on Cocaine Hill. He knew that picture was on all their minds by this stage.

But as with the long haul the day before back to the Brushy, the final stretch too took them longer than he had supposed. They weren't doing the obvious things properly any more: no one had thought to spell the outlaw horse that was packing double until it started to shake on its pins; and when they made the last mid-day camp past the old Indian town of Scullyville, he missed seeing his own mount's stone bruise. Both those small setbacks seemed like major disasters to them.

With one thing and another it was evening again before they crossed the Arkansas and turned slowly up First Street and past the gawking crowds there.

Even then there was a lengthy session of

paperwork at the courthouse in between them and those mirage beers.

TWELVE

Next morning the four of them filed into Judge Parker's private chambers and lined up in front of his desk.

The Judge had a full docket awaiting him downstairs that day; but he had unhesitatingly told his clerk to re-schedule court business so that he could personally congratulate the men who had brought Julius Kratoch back to face his verdict – and his vengeance.

He stroked his whitening goatee and gazed penetratingly at them all with his deep-socketed and very blue eyes. He knew far more about each one of them that they ever dreamt; as he did of most of his two hundred strong field force.

With due formality he directed his opening words to the officer who had headed the recapture detail.

"Deputy Cramer, you and the rest here have accomplished everything that the court asked of you in this matter. Indeed, perhaps a little over and above that," he added with a touch of dryness.

Bill Cramer shuffled a bit where he was standing. "If you mean about Laddy Huss and them other

135

bodies over their saddles, Your Honor, I can explain that as I done already in my report. Y'see –"

"Enough, enough," the jurist interrupted with a wave of his robed arm and a faint knowing smile. "I did not really suppose that men of your, umm, experience, would return here with only one criminal to show for your efforts – whatever your precise instructions were."

Cramer felt his face flushing up. Dammit, the old cuss was as good as accusing them that they'd gunned down Huss and those others to stack up some scalp money and make the run pay off …

But in fact Isaac Parker wasn't thinking that. He might have done, had Paul Monkerud not been along on the assignment. The Judge was certain, in his own highly religious mind, that one such as Monkerud would never have been a party to deliberate murder for any reason apart from fundamentalist passion. He was well aware that the tall and grim-faced deputy would do about anything else out of sheer greed; but not that.

His shrewd gaze shifted to fix now on the young one with the scorched head. The one who swore so disgracefully all the time. He shuttled his glance back at the impassive Monkerud. Yes, very likely there had been some salutary clash between those two …

Relaxing somewhat now that the first formalities had been observed, he said heartily: "Well, Huttman, how is the leg now? None the better for being bounced all over the Territory, eh?"

Slim gave him the sort of smile he usually kept in

reserve for bigwigs. "It ain't too bad now, Y'r Honor. Happen I kin ride again next time out, huh?" he grunted hopefully.

"We shall see, we shall see. That is a matter for the doctors to pronounce upon, not myself. However" – the odd blue eyes suddenly twinkled – "I know how you old cowboys regard culinary employment. We shall try to be, umm, merciful to you, Huttman."

Looking back at Cramer again: "You acted very properly by the unfortunate lady from McAlaster. Very properly indeed."

"I'm glad you say so, Your Honor. I mean, it seemed a mite hard on her, puttin' her in with the hunky." Cramer risked a slight chuckle as he seemed to be more or less in favor. "Hard on him too when she got in the habit of singin' at him toward the end of the run. She does that for a full hour every day, so she was tellin' us."

"Does she indeed. I, too, shall in my own way be singing to Mr Kratoch very shortly. *Yes, what is it now?*"

At that point there had come a knock on the door and an usher's harassed head now peered around it. "Court's ready and waiting to be upstanding, Your Honor."

"Very well, I shall be down directly."

He addressed himself finally to all four of them, cocking his head to one side in characteristic pose and allowing his true feelings to show through for the first time.

"I am deeply grateful to all of you for what you have achieved. As was promised to you at the outset,

I shall bear your dedication to the cause of justice
very much in mind when the time comes to review
your future careers in law enforcement. As for more
immediate and tangible reward, I confess I am glad
that Mr Huss and his associates have provided that
– even if it was not strictly in line with my
instructions!" He was twinkling again.

From the chambers door he looked back suddenly
and said: "Oh, and Cramer – I was so pleased to
hear the good news about your wife."

A last nod, and then they heard his long stride
going away.

* * *

"What'd he mean by that, Billy?" Slim wanted to
know when they had stepped downstairs and out
into the sunsmash.

Cramer grinned; the kind of wide grin that
stretched his cheek scar into a different shape
altogether. The kind of grin they hadn't seen on
him all the time they were out on the trip, or for a
good spell before that.

"Looks like Helen's sawn fit to come home," he
grunted with an elaborate shrug. "Had me a nice
supper waitin' last night when I got back to Tenth
Street, anyhow. We ain't said much yet. I figgered
best not to, not yet. I guess she tired of that
drummer and come home – or else he did of her."

"Howinhell did the old man git to know a private
thing like that?"

"Aw, what don't he know of in Smith. It's his

town."

They didn't exactly congratulate him, but Marvin punched his shoulder and Slim grinned back and even Paul allowed a ghost of a smile to lighten his usual sombre gravity.

As domestic life went for a federal deputy marshal, the ups and downs of Bill Cramer's weren't uncommon. The job loaded a sight of pressure on men and women alike. But if that part of it really went wrong, it tended to make a hard job an impossible one.

There was so little in the job besides; apart from being regularly shot and knifed and overworked, for very little pay. And that recent spiel they'd been given about 'bearing their dedication in mind' didn't cut much of a swath with them either. They each knew too well that even Isaac Parker couldn't do much for them when they reached wolf-bait age except maybe turn up some job as a lousy prairie sheriff. Or maybe one as a slightly less lousy prairie sheriff.

They went off together to hunt some more beer.

*   *   *

When the court rose at seven that evening, Judge Parker climbed the stairs tiredly to his chambers and tossed his robe over a chairback. He stretched out his tall frame with a deep yawn of relief.

Late sunlight was streaming in through the big corner window. Perhaps in order to enjoy its by now soft radiance upon his skin, he moved over to the glass and stood there looking down.

It was a very familiar pose of his. Below him, blindingly white in the sundown, stood the great twelve-man gallows that had made the Judge, Hangman Maledon, and Fort Smith itself, equally well-known names throughout the whole country. And at this precise moment he was wistfully picturing Julius Kratoch swinging there from the massive crossbeam.

But, of course, the wretched Bohemian had committed no capital offense that would allow him to place him there; more by luck than management, if this recent spree in the Territory was anything to go by. But an indisputable fact nevertheless. He couldn't hang the fellow and, despite all these recent shenanigans, he doubted that he could lawfully add much more to his original intention of committing him to the government prison in Ohio for the liquor offense.

A contradictory impulse now took sway over Isaac Parker's complex nature. He'd taken a quick look at Kratoch in the cells after they'd brought him back last night, and had been shocked by what he'd seen of his present condition. To send a man in that state to a climate like Ohio's would be a death sentence in itself, of a kind he didn't favor.

And yet, by thunder, he *still wanted to punish him* for all the trouble and loss of dignity he had caused him by the cool nerve of that break for freedom!

Then there was the sheer administrative problem to consider of reconvening Kratoch's trial. *Had* a trial ever been reconvened at such a late juncture? He could think of no precedent, however far he cast his mind back through the encylopedia of criminal law that was contained in it. And that aside, what of the practical difficulty of re-summoning the jury, now doubtless dispersed far and wide over the whole of western Arkansas?

By now he was almost beginning to regret having sent the tumbleweed team after Julius Kratoch in the first place. The sheer temper which had driven him to that had long since been dispelled by the strains and stresses of following cases – some of them much more serious than the whiskey runner's.

He just did not know what to do about him next. He realized that he wanted somehow to be both hard and soft on him at one and the same time; with precious little chance of managing either. It was really most vexing …

Isaac Parker uttered a sudden groan as he remembered a lesser vexation that he felt he should attend to today before casting off the cares of his high office: the matter of this unlucky Frenchwoman who had been caught up in Kratoch's sordid affairs.

… Yes, on his way home now to North Thirteenth he really should go by way of the Leflore Hotel, where he understood the lady was staying while her departure was being arranged. He would just stop by and pay his respects and, perhaps, offer to assist her in some small way if that seemed merited. In the circumstances that courtesy was clearly incumbent on him.

Sighing, he went to freshen up and brush his suit before attending to this last and self-imposed chore of the day.

THIRTEEN

Oren Stone, the manager of the LeFlore, snatched the rum-cured cigar from his thick lips when he saw who it was coming in the foyer. He also buttoned up his wine-coloured velvet waistcoat over his big belly as he hastened forward.

Isaac Parker hadn't been inside these portals since around last Christmas, when the hotel had hosted a dinner of the Fort Smith Bar Association. That was the only type of gathering that was likely to cause the austere and home-loving Judge to enter the town's premier hostelry. Orrie Stone couldn't figure what had fetched him here now.

The reason was soon made known to him. As soon as he had greeted Parker at the foot of the small-scale 'Windsor' staircase the Judge said: "Yes, I am in good health, thank you, Stone ... but what, pray, is that noise I hear?" The famous blue eyes were looking up the stairs in some alarm.

Stone gave an apologetic grin. "It's the Frenchwoman, Your Honor. Her off the tumbleweed. It appears she's some kind of chanteuse. She does it by the hour up there. I haven't said nothing, not seeing it's a slack time for us just now and I've had no complaints yet, but if you'd like for me to tell her to shut it I'll go do that right away, Judge."

"That will not be necessary, Stone," Parker murmured, wincing a little and resolutely mounting the stairs. "In fact it is Madame de Duras that I have come to see. Do you think this will be a convenient time for me to call on her?"

"Sure thing, Judge," Orrie Stone responded automatically. The hotel man couldn't conceive of any time of day being unwelcome for a visiting stage woman to receive the singular honor of a call from Fort Smith's leading citizen. And, if he were being honest with himself, neither could the Judge imagine that very easily.

He carried on up the elaborate short staircase, the pinched expression on his face increasing as he climbed.

... What in thunderation did this racket remind him of? It certainly made him think of something. Then he nailed it: the sound of the brass firehorn, when there was that big waterfront blaze two years back ... He braced himself and knocked on the hallway door nearest to those sounds.

It was snatched irritably open. "Yes, what is it? I am busy."

Charlotte de Duras eyed the large and embarrassed figure in the doorway without interest. She had had a bath at the LeFlore and removed the last of the tar and feathers from her thick and now plainly reddish hair. She had also purchased a pale blue organdie dress in the town, with lace trimming and fashionable puff sleeves. (And with a bodice line that the jurist immediately thought of as *racy*, which had been the phrase in vogue for that kind of thing when he was a young man.) There was a blue ribbon pinned in her hair. Although smarter than before, she still contrived to look bohemian, in the sense of that word which Julius Kratoch emphatically was not. All in all she was pretty much in line with the straight-laced Judge's idea of a stage woman.

"Madame, pray forgive this intrusion," he began with a stiff smile. "I am Isaac Parker. I believe you accompanied some of my men back here from the Territory, after an unfortunate *contretemps* with some of our Indians there. I just thought that I would see how you go on – and enquire if I may assist you in any way as regards your return to, ahem, civilization."

He felt rather pleased with slipping in that *contretemps*. However, he had not much more French at his command and hoped that wouldn't be required of him. He began to feel uneasy on that score as the lady made no reply at first.

Then, suddenly, she said in accusing tones: "You are the Hanging Judge, yes? The man who seeks to hang poor Julius! The man who *persecutes the sick*!" She glared at him.

He was taken aback by this unexpected verbal assault. Finally he choked out: "Well, yes, it is true I have been called that by certain newspapers – by certain sensational newspapers. As to Kratoch, I have no intention of hanging him, I do assure you!

His offense is not a capital one." His tone quietened down to a more conversational level. "I gather you became acquainted with the fellow during your, umm, unavoidable journey together. I do sincerely regret that, madame. It is not pleasant to have to associate with criminals, as I know but too well myself ..." He paused, still displaying an air of marked uneasiness and affront.

Charlotte took a sharper look at her large and formidable visitor. It occurred to her that this hanging judge was not at all as she had pictured him from Julius's bitter description while they were together. In fact, he was plainly a person of some culture and refinement. Perhaps she was not behaving over-well toward him ...

"Would you step inside for a moment, sir? Forgive me if I was blunt. I am upset over Julius, that is the reason."

The Judge hesitated and then complied. He found himself in one of the LeFlore's lesser rooms, and as he sat down there he said punctiliously to her: "Dear me, Stone should be doing better by you than this, madame. Especially as I understand the hotel is by no means full now."

She made an impatient gesture from the settee where she had seated herself. "Oh, I don't mind where I find myself. In my profession one learns to adapt at an early age." She gave a short bellow of laughter. "At a much earlier age than mine!" She peered at him curiously. "Are you yourself, perhaps, at all inclined to the stage?"

He shook his white head indulgently. "I find that

husbanding the law is not a task that permits much in the way of outside interest. When I was a young Congressman in Washington I now and then found time for the playhouse. But now – no, hardly ever. Not that my profession is lacking in its own theatrics," he added in a musing way. "Sometimes I think we have more than enough of it!" He chuckled politely. "You must forgive me for my philistinism."

"So, yes, a little theatre once – but no music ever, eh?" Charlotte said severely. "My mother did *Lucia* in Washington. But I suppose you would not have seen that performance."

"Alas, no, for I am quite unmusical and always have been." He recalled her singing just now and was privately grateful to God for that deficiency.

"Julius is quite musical – or, at least, I was teaching him to be more appreciative than he seemed at the start of our friendship."

He gave her a puzzled stare, then dismissed that odd way of putting it as just feminine prattle. She had reminded him of his own serious dilemma over the whiskey runner and he shook his head sadly.

"Where he is bound for there is not much point in teaching him anything, I fear. You see the poor man is most unlikely to survive his next prison sentence."

Charlotte looked at him in surprise. Like many a stranger to Isaac Parker before her, she was making the strange discovery that the Hanging Judge had a strong streak of compassion. She was intrigued, and in her extrovert and impulsive way she moved closer to him from where she was sitting. "Would you care for some refreshment, sir?"

"Oh no, really, for I am on my way home to my supper. In any event I never take alcohol."

Her large lace-edged hand hovered over the small bell on the table by her. "I was thinking of just some tea and cream perhaps?"

"Thank you but no."

They sat in thoughtful silence together. Parker felt more at ease with her now. There was something beginning to stir at the back of his mind; he didn't yet know what.

"That man is a confounded nuisance," he remarked suddenly.

"Poor Julius, you mean?"

"Poor Julius be blowed! Do you know that he actually stood on me – *on me* – to effect his escape from the courtroom? And do you know also that your poor Julius has made a career out of driving my poor Indians out of their senses with raw whiskey?"

Charlotte nodded decisively. "There is no question that all that sort of thing has got to stop. And his smoking also. It is sheerly ridiculous, a man in that parlous condition indulging in tobacco."

Isaac Parker studied her for a long moment with his head dropping down slowly toward his shoulder. Then he said: "Four prison terms have entirely failed to stop his criminal activity in the Territory, madame. As to the other deprivation you have in mind, I doubt that would be any easier to impose.

Tuberculosis patients are often most perverse heavy smokers, I believe."

"That is because they are allowed to be! What Julius needs is deep breathing. Ultimately, as much as a thousand deep breaths a day, as the muscles grow stronger. I have already started him in that direction, and made him see the value of it. As for his ... bootlegging, is that the word? – he has told me what his returns were from it and they were not impressive. I have explained to him that there are much more profitable avenues open to a man of continental culture. What he needs is firm direction toward a position connected with the arts – perhaps most suitably in a business capacity."

She broke off and looked challengingly at the Judge. "If he were a free man I would unhesitatingly employ him as my business manager. I need such a manager badly at this stage in my life. The wretched affair in McAlester would never have happened if my affairs had been properly handled. I am an artiste, and that is exacting enough in all conscience. I have no time or capacity to be my own manager besides."

It was quite preposterous, of course ... but in the profound silence which followed Judge Parker was imagining a future for Kratoch in which both bootlegging and smoking were simply not allowed; but which did include a compulsory thousand deep breaths each day, plus a hardly avoidable requirement that he listened to Madam de Duras's scales practice for one hour in every twenty-four until the end of his life.

Was it really so preposterous? Did it not rather, in actual fact, perfectly answer his own impossible desire to sentence Kratoch both harshly and yet also with due mercy and regard to his condition?

That most onerous sentence would certainly deal well enough with the scoundrel who had stood on his head, he told himself firmly; provided that specific safeguards could be established. He now cautiously began to do that.

"Do you yourself enjoy good health, madame?" (Which was a way of asking if the jailer could reasonably be expected to outlast her singular ward of court.)

"Oh yes, sir, I am as strong as an ox. For what I do one has to be."

"Umm. You will forgive me but I am cynical as to stage partnerships. In my experience they are often held together by no more than financial expediency. In short, they tend not to last. Something more – definite would be needed in a case of this kind." He regarded her steadily.

Charlotte took the point with her usual brisk straightforwardness.

"Oh, I would marry him, if that is what you mean!"

"Ah: but would he marry you? I have known this jailbird for rather longer than you have. He is stubborn, as I have been trying to explain."

She stared at him with a kind of perplexed irritation. "But why ever should he not? *He* is no catch! I just happen to take to him! Why should he possibly object? Who else is liable to bother with him?"

The Judge was now feeling slightly shocked. He had realized that the lady was not precisely romantic in her designs upon Kratoch; but even so, there were certain proprieties to be observed – even in this remarkable conversation. But he stuck gamely to his guns.

"Have you ever been married before? There would be no, umm, complications?"

"Oh no. There was no time for that earlier. Even as a child, and then as a young girl, I was always working on the music. Now I have reached the point where I require a manager: and if it is simpler that he is my husband also, that is OK. Julius would suit me very well – out of jail, of course! What good is he to himself or to anyone else in jail? None whatever."

Judge Parker was now finally reaching that conclusion himself. But he was more aware than Julius Kratoch's intended seemed to be that their common objective might take some careful contriving to bring about.

"You were saying he fears that I'll hang him … Why is that? He knows more than most that whiskey peddling is not a capital crime."

"Oh, he has a fixed belief that those men who attacked the wagon, those other Czechs whom your men killed, will have made it certain that he is hanged, on top of the manner of his escape from custody before." She gave an incredulous laugh. "He really thinks you have the power of life and death over everyone in this town, sir."

He made no answer to that. In the past, back in Fort Smith's frontier time, that had been truer than the lady realized. Nowadays, though, there were several restrictions placed upon his absolute power by the Congress and the Supreme Court. And there had always been certain inviolable restrictions that he had placed upon himself: if any of his deputies had been killed, or even suffered mild injury while retaking Kratoch, he would never have considered what had been discussed here this evening.

He rose toweringly to take his leave. "I take it then, madame, that you will be remaining here in the city for a while until this matter is, umm, resolved?"

Fort Smith was still nothing approaching a 'city' to the much-travelled Charlotte de Duras; but she quickly sensed that it would be a mistake to let that opinion of it show to the strange and complex man who was so unexpectedly falling in with her plans – and even making them for her now.

She got up too and told him gravely: "Yes, sir, I shall remain in the city until the matter is resolved."

He nodded down at her with approval, and his vivid eyes suddenly twinkled. Then he bowed and went out.

FOURTEEN

At the noon adjournment next day he ate a hasty sandwich in his chambers and then had Kratoch brought up to him there. "Wait outside the door," he told the two escort guards. Then he put the stark choice before the Bohemian: – hanging or an indefinite custodial sentence with Madame de Duras.

Julius Kratoch's treacherous-looking flecked eyes opened wide with amazement and then he made a sound that was half a lung cough and half a cry of desperation.

"Jesus Christ, Y'r Honor ... I can't do it. Not to that one I can't."

"Why not? Have you a wife already?"

"Have I hell. Ain't I found enough trouble without that?"

"Why not, then?" He fixed him with a steady judical stare.

"Because I don't shine up to her, that's why not!" Kratoch flung back at him with a show of courage and yellow teeth.

"Umm. I doubt that the lady is attached to you

153

in precisely that fashion herself. But she does require a business manager for her musical career. Were you to take up her, ahem, general offer, Kratoch, I should warn you that you will find her opposed to your favourite habit of introducing spirituous liquors into the Indian Nations. I understand also that madame does not approve of smoking in her presence. And then, as you already know, she has various health measures in mind for you – purely for your benefit," he said blandly.

"Now, man, which is it to be: that or the noose? Make up your mind for I haven't got all day."

Kratoch raised a shaking hand to his forehead and gazed around wildly at the big window in the corner of the room. The Judge gave a wry snort.

"You'd better not try to jump out of *that*, since it is closed and also well above ground. I fancy you would both cut your throat and break your neck, in rapid succession. And if by some miracle you were unhurt you would still be placed most conveniently near to the gallows."

Kratoch licked his lips and shaped them in the familiar snarl.

"You got no right to hang me without a trial. I mean a new trial. You know damn well I never done nothin' capital till Ladi Huss went and provoked all that killin' on the prairie. That killin' weren't my fault, 'cept mebbe in your crazy law books. Why, it never even caused your marshals to git lead up their asses, like my shotgun didn't neither. I demand a new trial!"

"I'm tired of presiding over your trials," Isaac

Parker told him sincerely. "I would remind you that I have total jurisdiction in this federal court. If I decide you'll hang, Kratoch – believe me you will."

The prisoner stood there before him at his desk, swaying slightly and with his wan bony face twisting with emotion. The jurist felt a spasm of shame to be doing this to him; but resolutely ignored it.

"No, I won't be whipsawed, Judge," Kratoch wheezed finally. "I won't wed her and that's it. I've had a bait of the whiskey business now anyway without her say-so, believe it or not. And I'm not sayin' she's a bad-intentioned woman in herself. She knows a thing or two I don't. And I guess I wouldn't mind handlin' her stage doings and seeing she don't get herself tar-and-feathered and that kind of foolishness. But none a that counts since I couldn't live with her, Judge. You ain't had her singin' at you like I have … and she does it fer a full hour every day." He gave a visible shudder. "I jes' knows I couldn't stand it."

Isaac Parker's instinctive surge of sympathy at that point very nearly overbore his determination to carry this through. But fortunately Kratoch's own words were now encouraging him and steeling him to his purpose.

He hadn't supposed that he would persuade him just through his own eloquence; another kind of eloquence altogether was now needed.

"So be it, then." He gave a helpless hand-flourish and got up from the desk and went to the door in two of his giant strides. "Deputy Simmons: find Mr Maledon and ask him to step up here for a moment, will you?"

Julius Kratoch had lost a little colour in a way that had nothing to do with his illness. "You mean like *today*, Judge?"

"Why not today, if it's convenient? Better than brooding over it! Oh, it will have to depend on Maledon's schedules," he told him offhandedly. He picked up some court papers and began to study them while they waited.

That was not for long; though it seemed so to Julius Kratoch. When the door opened the next time he gave an audible swallow.

"Ah, Maledon, there you are!"

The stocky and bushy-bearded court hangman entered the room with a quiet "Howdy, Judge." Parker had deliberated earlier whether he could be told a little about his plan, to ensure that the next crucial part of it was effective. But he had decided against that. The little Bavarian was no play actor. It was better just to let him be himself.

"Now, Maledon, I know how busy you are just now, but if you could arrange to accommodate Mr Kratoch here some time today I should be most grateful."

George Maledon took a quick squint at Julius Kratoch and then looked shrewdly at the Judge. It was no surprise to him that Isaac was hurting for the bohunk to be stretched now he'd gotten him back. He growled casually: "Today, huh? Well, there's a space around five when I could mebbe fit

him in. That's if there ain't no special difficulties
with this here subject."

With an air of professional concentration he
began to shamble in a small and close circle around
the subject concerned. Kratoch's bugging eyes tried
to turn with him, cork-screwing his head around,
until the executioner said softly: "Hold still now,
hunky."

The wiry beard brushed against Kratoch's skin as
he took a closer look at that jaw. Then, shaking his
grizzled head and still inspecting his subject with
dissatisfaction, he backed away from him and stood
near the Judge with folded arms. He often stood
like that when up on the scaffold.

"Well, Mr Maledon?"

"I dunno, Your Honor. A chin like that there,
when you take it together with the full length I'll
need to use what with him bein' light anyway, and
now gone lighter still from sickness ... I'm not
sayin' it's beyond me to keep the subject's head on
but I sure can't promise to."

He was warming to this technical challenge now,
his droning guttural voice carrying clearly across to
the stricken Czech. "... then there's how to set the
brass bit to give us the best result. I'd like to tuck it
plumb under a jaw like that – but we mustn't fergit
there's big blood lines there. We don't want a mess
on the platform which I sure-hell won't have time to
git scrubbed off for them Allen boys who'll be due
to come up to me straight after him ... Nah, I'll
have to set the brass eye nighward of that there jaw,
and just hope that don't –"

A long and soul-riven scream had burst forth from Julius Kratoch and cut short the hangman's expert appraisal.

"All right, Judge! All right! I'll do it! You kin have the banns put up! Do what you damn like! – *only keep your pet buzzard away from me!*"

George Maledon looked back at him with faint surprise, and with the first ordinary interest he'd taken in him since entering the chambers.

Of course, he was quite accustomed to subjects yelling out all sorts of loco'd stuff when they were getting close to the Time. But that stuff about banns was a new one. He wondered if it was maybe just hunky talk.

The Judge tapped him on the shoulder. "Thank you, Mr Maledon – thank you very much. When you go out please ask those two on the door to take Kratoch back to his cell now. And, umm, you can leave him out of your schedule for today after all.'

* * *

Four days later, Marvin Pollins lurched excitably into a colored bar in the town and headed for the mournful-drunk figure of Slim Huttman which was sagging on one of the stools. Cramer and Monkerud were out in the field again by then on new assignments.

"Slimmy, snap alive! You'd never guess in a million years what I just saw! Why, madame an' the hunky, comin' out of Saint Thingy's with their hair full of rice, that's what! An' the hunky all duded in black broadcloth with a pearl pin this big!

"Well, nacherally, I gits to thinkin' he's stood on the Judge agin, and mebbe grabbed the suit off his back as well this time as he gone by him! So I crosses the street at a dead run and pulls my iron and shoves it in his brisket!

"But then madame just sorta grins at me and says – you know that certain way she talks – she says: *It is perfectly in order, Deputy*. And then she says: *Come, Julius, the carriage is waiting*.

"Then they both climb on the rig and damned if that no-account whiskey runner don't say to Art Mellor on the seat: *The railroad station, my good man!*

'Slimmy, I swear on my life all this is true as we're settin' here."

Slim Huttman nodded. "Sure it's true. I seen that comin' a mile off. Smart ol' woman, that madame."

He paused, and looked out morosely through the plate glass window toward the river. "Smart ol' hunky too ..."